THE SEDUCTION OF LUNA

A Steamy Past Lives Romance

VIOLET HAZE

Stoked Publishing House

Cover Design from BookCoverZone
Stoked Publishing House

ISBN-13: 978-0-9992261-3-1
Independently Published
April 2019

CHAPTER ONE

"See something you like?"

The man stares at me like I'm a sweet piece of candy he's been denying himself for so long, he plans to take a big bite out of me as soon as he can.

My intention is to let him fuck me four ways to Sunday when we get back to his place, which is quite fitting considering it's Saturday night.

"You bet."

I grin at his response, delight and excitement coursing through me at the devilish gleam in his gorgeous blue-green eyes. That's when his eyes drop from their initial connection with mine to my barely covered cleavage.

A strategic move on my part as no man seems able to keep their focus off them for long.

He lifts a hand and rests it on my bare shoulder, the

warm contact of his palm against my skin setting it to sizzling. It has been a few days since someone touched me and I'm on edge because I need it.

No, I *crave* the touch of a lover.

When he leans in, seeking access to my neck, I oblige with a tilt of my head, even though we're in a booth in the middle of a restaurant. I don't care about being in public. This little interlude will only go so far before neither of us want to wait any longer for the real show to begin.

A few minutes to let him have a taste and leave him wanting more because I want him touching me everywhere tonight, fulfilling my desires.

I yearn for his lips to take mine, force my mouth open and plunder it with so much force that when he drags his mouth away, I'm gasping for breath. One hand will be on my breast while the other slides down and slips into my panties, seeking my pussy. And when I move my hips, trying to coax the hand to go further, he'll laugh and pull away enough to elicit a curse from me.

Right now, though, he places a few tame kisses on my neck and draws back, his smirk lopsided rather than suggestive.

"What's your name, pretty girl?"

I barely restrain an eye-roll at his calling me *girl* because at twenty-three, with measurements of 36-32-38 on a toned five-foot-seven frame, I'm definitely all woman.

"Call me Luna." I slide my right hand under the table to rest it on his leg. "What's yours?"

He winks and lifts his beer to tip it at me. "Rick."

After he takes a swing and places the bottle back on the table, I glide my hand upward and smile.

"Well, Rick." Saying his name with a drawl, I chuckle a bit at hearing him let out a hiss between his teeth as my hand moves closer to his trouser-covered cock. "How about we take this party back to your place?"

His hand shoots beneath the table, grabbing mine a second before it makes contact. I pout in protest, mainly for show even though he doesn't know that, which leads him to lift my hand to his lips and kiss my knuckles.

"We've just met." He releases his grip on my hand and takes another drink. "Are you sure you want to go already?"

"Yes."

I don't say anything else. I don't need to.

Why would I when he's a stranger and we only met thirty minutes ago. He saw me dining alone and invited me to join him at his table. An invitation to flirt and one I gladly accepted, hopeful of taking things to the next level quickly.

That is the whole reason I sit alone in restaurants, dressing in a provocative manner because my tactics work every single time. Offers to join single men at their tables never takes longer than thirty minutes top, typically because most are waiting to see if anyone — basically, another man — is planning to join me.

So yeah, no need to give them an explanation because I get what I want in the end, which is all I care about.

Rick takes care of the bill and stands, holding out a hand to help me rise, which I accept graciously.

"I'm staying here," he says as we walk toward the lobby. "I'm visiting from out of town."

Damn, this just keeps getting better and better. I try to keep the joy out of my voice at this revelation. "When do you leave?"

"Tomorrow." He frowns at me. "You?"

Realizing he thinks I'm also a guest here, I use it to my advantage as the elevator doors open, since this means we likely won't ever cross paths again. "Same. I'm just here for the night."

We step inside and the doors close, punctuating our unspoken agreement to spend the evening in each other's arms before parting in the morning, never to see each other again.

Exactly the way I like it.

THE CLOCK STRIKES SEVEN AS I EXIT THE HOTEL.

Rick must've had an early flight because when I awoke,

he was gone. While dressing to leave, I noticed something on the nightstand, discovering a business card he left behind with his personal number on it.

Apparently he thought I might call him and get together again if he was ever in town again. I threw the card in the trash without a second thought even though the sex was great because the man certainly was an attentive lover.

However, I don't have sex with anyone more than once. It is one night and done; most weren't worth a second time anyway. I know that sucks for those who are great and might entertain me for more than a night, but there are no exceptions.

And now, the time has come to walk home from the hotel. This is my pick-up place of choice because I don't live far.

Not even half a mile away is my townhouse, which I share with my two roommates and best friends from college, Iris and Dexter.

My high heel snaps, jerking me away from my thoughts, and I topple forward. My palms scrape against the ground as I catch myself, releasing a hiss through my teeth from the instant pain.

Rolling toward my back, I sit up on the payment and pick up the shoe, checking out the damage before I smack it repeatedly on the ground in frustration. "Fuck!"

It takes a second for me to notice that a sleek, shiny

black car has stopped next to the curb. I glance up and freeze, scowling at the smile creeping across the man's face.

He's taken off his seatbelt and is leaning across the middle of the vehicle to keep me in his view. "You won't break ground by using a shoe. You do know that, don't you?"

At his mirth filled observation, I throw my shoe at the open window and he ducks, making sure it flies past his head before landing inside the car somewhere.

He chuckles and steps out, leaving the car idling as he walks over to offer me a hand up.

That's when I realize who the man is and — thank fuck — he doesn't recognize me in my short-haired brown wig. I'm also wearing color contacts, but I highly doubt he's ever taken note of my eye color when he comes into my work.

Accepting his hand, I wince as my raw palm meets his and stand up. Letting go immediately, I gently kick my other shoe off and bend my knees to pick it up.

I rack my brain, trying to remember his name, and fail. Every time he's at the diner, he orders a black coffee and a bowl of mixed fruit, then sits at the table for an hour while reading the newspaper; a routine he's kept up for over a month now.

When I finally meet his dark chocolate gaze with my fake green one, he grins and gestures to his car. "May I give you a ride to wherever you need to go?"

Shaking my head, I step back and nod toward the direction of my place. "No, thanks. I'm not far from here."

Shit. Why did I say that? For all I know, he could be a stalker, and now he knows I live nearby!

He looks down at my feet, then back up at my face. "You aren't wearing any shoes; you could hurt yourself."

"I'll be fine." Insistent on doing things for myself, as always, I start walking with the hope he doesn't follow me.

He offers again. "Why don't you let me at least drop you really close by? I'll even drive away and you can watch me go before heading to your building."

Whirling around, I cross my arms over my chest and huff. "I don't even know your name. I'm not getting into your car with you because you could kidnap me and—"

"Tobias Giles-Blackburn." Cutting in, he takes out his wallet and flips it open to show me his driver's license. "I'm not going to kidnap you. Even if I wanted to, now you know my name, so I'd have to kill you to keep you silent, and I'm wearing my best suit."

My mouth drops open at his statement, even as I acknowledge that his ensemble — a light grey three-piece suit and white undershirt with a red tie for a pop of color — flatters his physique and features quite well.

"I saw you fall, and all I want to do is help." He walks over to the car and opens the passenger door. "Now, are you going to get in or what?"

Snapping my mouth shut, I look to the right and

consider my options. Right now, we're at least a quarter mile away from my place, quite a long walk for me shoeless. I will have to walk slowly and watch the ground to make sure there isn't any injury to the bottom of my feet if I don't accept his offer.

Not something I want to deal with this morning.

"Fine." Sighing, I walk the few steps until only the passenger door separates us and hold up my shoe, heel out. "But don't try anything funny. I may not be able to break ground with this, but I'm definitely capable of puncturing your face with it."

He laughs and leans close until our noses nearly touch. "Not to worry. While I enjoy a little feistiness in the bedroom, the only time I ignore a 'no' is when there's a consensual safe-word in place."

I'm not shocked at his words. I know all about kink and the various forms of enjoyment it can bring to the bedroom. Instead of responding like he obviously wants me to, I slide onto the seat and question him as he goes to shut the door.

"Don't you want to know the name of the woman you've invited into your car?"

He shrugs. "Only if you want to tell me."

Before I can respond, the door clicks shut and he walks around to climb in the driver's seat. He puts on his seatbelt, then turns his head my way and just smiles at me.

"What?"

He tilts his head a little, pointing a finger at his own restraint. "Can't drive 'til you put it on."

"We're going two minutes down the road!"

"A lot can happen in those couple'a minutes."

Irritated, I grab the belt and put it on with an annoyed snap. "Is that a line you use on every woman you meet?"

He ignores my remark and pulls away from the curb, laughing. "Where do you want me to drop you off?"

I want to glare at him, but why the hell am I so pissed off at a man who just wants to help me?

Taking a deep breath, I point ahead at a spot two houses down from my place. "You can let me out by that driveway, with the green trash can at the end of it."

Within what feels like seconds, he pulls into the driveway and once he puts the car in park, I open the door.

"Thanks for the ride."

As I go to step out, he puts a hand on mine, halting me. "Wait."

The tingle of awareness shoots up my arm as his hand covers mine and my thighs clench together. Hoping he doesn't notice my reaction, I lift a brow and smirk while waiting for him to continue with whatever he wants to say.

"You never told me your name."

I blink, not expecting him to ask considering his remark earlier about telling him being my decision. Maybe he wants to ask me out on a date, and yes, knowing my name is certainly the first step to doing that.

There's no question of whether I should tell him my real name. I never do that because I'm uninterested in anything long-term and without my disguise, I'm merely Jocelyn, the woman nobody notices unless I'm taking their order or make a mistake.

When I lick my lips, unsure of whether I should leave him wondering or not, his gaze drops to watch and my decision is made.

I want to fuck him, which means he'll know me the same way other men do. I stick my hand out, and he clasps it in his, eyes filled with desire as I finally introduce myself. "Luna."

"Well, Luna, how about dinner tomorrow?"

There's no reason to deny him now. Not when I've decided we're going to have sex for the hell of it. I accept his invitation with a nod.

He shakes his head, gives my hand a sharp tug to pull me toward him, and slides his free hand around my head to cradle the nape of my neck.

Our lips meet even as his boldness makes me gasp, although this show of his dominance is secretly thrilling. He doesn't seek entrance with his tongue, merely keeps the sweet kiss as one meant to promise more after we're finished with dinner tomorrow evening.

He pulls away, moving both his hands back to the steering wheel, and winks at me. "We'll meet at seven in the hotel lobby."

Struck speechless by the way his kiss set my body on fire, I mentally slap myself out of it and open the door. "See you at seven."

Stepping out of the car, I close the door and watch him drive off, all while smiling like a fool.

CHAPTER TWO

THE NEXT MORNING HE WALKS INTO MY DINER AS PER his habit every Monday. Afraid he will recognize me by voice alone, I grab the arm of one of my two employees and pull her inside the kitchen area.

"I need you to take care of him today." The request is delivered in what I want to consider is a calm and collected whisper. "Tell him I'm sick if he asks for me."

As the boss, I have to display complete confidence to those who work for me. If I panic, they will follow, and that's never good for business. Not that we're doing all that well in the first place, so keeping every customer happy is a top priority around here.

Molly grins because she loves serving the men she considers handsome. "No problem." She gives me a wink before heading through the doors to do as asked.

I don't know what bothers me more: the fact she

doesn't even question why I wasn't taking care of him myself like always, or if her jubilant and enthusiastic acceptance of my request means she's gonna take this chance to hit on him.

Doesn't take long for her to return, though, this time with a perplexed look that makes my stomach clench.

"Something wrong?"

"Ah, he asked me where you were and said he's a creature of habit. He prefers you serve him."

Dammit.

I don't realize I've actually said the word until Molly's mouth drops open, a reaction she quickly covers with a grimace. "I told him you were sick. He said it didn't matter to him, and he wants you taking his order."

I'll bet he does!

Patting her shoulder, I shove the thought aside because nobody tells me what to do, but again, he's a customer. "Thanks for trying. Go get the customer who just walked in for me instead."

She takes off with a nod.

Running my hands over my head, I ensure my black hair is still wrapped neat and smooth in a bun, then slide them down the front of my clothing in the hopes of being most presentable.

What am I doing?

He wants to sleep with me as Luna, not Jocelyn Bates, the girl who serves him breakfast three days a week.

There's no way he'll make the connection if he hasn't already, yet here I stand primping like a high school girl preparing to go on a first date with a hot and popular classmate.

Get a grip, Bates!

As I walk toward him, pad and pen in hand, I can't help but admire him. He's wearing a suit, as always. Today's choice is dark blue pinstripe with white collared shirt and a complementary blue tie. His dark brown hair is windblown, his cheeks flushed as he sits with his hands folded on the table, waiting patiently.

All that changes as I approach, his dark eyes meeting my natural grey-blue ones, and he smiles.

I freeze, breath stolen as I remember my response to his kiss yesterday.

What the fuck is wrong with me? I've never had such a visceral reaction to anyone in my life.

Maybe it's his glorious smile. He has straight white teeth surrounded by lips that are neither too big nor too plump. Perfect teeth to go along with the perfect mouth that briefly touched mine yesterday and will be licking me all over later this evening.

Well, that is my plan, at least.

"Are you all right?"

I jerk my eyes up to his, face flaming because he's been speaking to me, and I haven't heard a word. Nervous, I lick my lips and smile back, even though I'm certain there's more to the feeling than I'm willing to think about.

"Yes, sorry. Would you like your usual?" I don't know why I don't just bring the coffee and bowl of fruit with me when he's here. His order never differs; he's a creature of habit, as he had told Molly not even a few minutes ago.

I can't blame him for wanting me to serve him, though. Since the first day he walked in, I've refused to let anyone else serve him; in hindsight, perhaps that hadn't been the smartest decision.

He removes his hands from the table and leans back against the seat. As he stares at me, his brows lower, mouth twisted a little at whatever thoughts are running through his mind.

My heart speeds up as I wait for his answer, afraid the jig is up before I've even gotten the chance to get him naked.

Will recognition flare in his eyes? Will his lips say the name I gave him yesterday and completely blow any chance of us having sex?

"No." He finally replies after crossing his arms over his chest. "I want to know what you believe is the best breakfast item on the menu. What do you recommend?"

I blink once. Twice. "I don't eat here."

His eyes widen. That probably isn't the best answer I could have given him because why I eat here has nothing to do with the food quality, so I'll clarify. "What I mean is—"

There's an indecipherable gleam in his eye as he cuts in. "Why not? Is the food here not edible?"

"No!" My spine stiffens, my eyes narrowing because it seems as if he's intent on proving something and frankly, he's keeping me from helping any other customers. "I mean, yes, it is. The fact I don't here has nothing to do with whether the food is good or not."

"If you don't eat here, how do you know it is good?"

"Because I own this place and wouldn't serve crap to anyone."

"Interesting." He sits back against the seat once more. "So, tell me what you believe is the best breakfast food here, then."

"Why is that interesting? Did you not know I'm the owner?"

He chuckles. "Of course, I do. I've also wondered why you serve customers since that is a job usually left to a waitress."

"Because..." Lowering my voice, I place my palms flat on the table and lean in so he can hear me, hoping the other diners remain oblivious to my sudden annoyance. "I believe in doing my fair share around here beyond the paperwork. And I believe in making sure every single customer is satisfied to my fullest ability."

He sits up and moves his face close enough that our

noses nearly touch. Gathering he expects me to pull away, I resist the urge and stay put.

"Is that a promise, Ms. Bates?"

I'm more than annoyed now. Not only is he questioning the food in my restaurant, but he's so close the sweet and fresh scent of his cologne assaults my senses. For the first time in my life, I want to slap someone almost as much as I want to fuck them.

Guess there's a first time for everything.

"No, that's a damn guarantee." I hiss this at him, straightening again to pull out my pad and pen as his grin widens. "If you must know, I recommend the french toast. We use bread made from scratch—"

He interrupts me once more. "Do you have a sister?"

I quell the instant panic that fills me and scowl instead. "No! Why? Would you wanna insult her, too?"

"Don't be so dramatic." He looks down at his watch, then back up at me. "You just remind me of someone I met yesterday and kind of sound like her too."

My mouth drops open.

How do I *kind* of sound like myself?

Speaking before thinking it through probably isn't the best idea even as the words leaves my mouth. "Oh, do I? Does she think you're an impudent jackass, too?"

He surprises me by laughing. "Probably." Clearing his throat, he looks me straight in the eye. "Sorry about that. I'll take that french toast and some coffee, please."

I nod and write it down, then twirl on my heel and walk away.

He calls out to me. "Oh, and Ms. Bates?"

I stop and wait without turning around.

"I hope you feel better soon."

I wince inwardly, knowing he's pointing out how sick I'm not, but lift a hand in acknowledgment and head to the kitchen.

"IRIS! COME HERE FOR A SEC, PLEASE?"

I'm standing in front of the mirror, putting my wig in place when she walks , and turn at her whistle of appreciation.

Iris has been my best friend since we were five years old. We attended the same school from kindergarten through college. When we got this place, we were afraid that living together would end up ruining our friendship, since that was the sort of thing people told us would happen.

But it hasn't.

I think it is because we are — and always have been — two very different people. She is stubborn; I'm less so. I'm passive while she's more aggressive. She likes relationships; I don't. On and on. We each do our own thing, being there for each other no matter what, with no judgment.

"What do you think?"

My black layer skirt falls to right above my knees, my silk shirt is emerald-colored with a deep v-neck, and my pumps are black as well. I've put on eyeliner, matching eye shadow, and lip gloss. With my wig and contacts, I look nothing like mousy Jocelyn who goes make-up free and wears drab outfits.

Iris smiles at me, her blue eyes shining. "You look gorgeous as always. But—"

I shake my head. "Don't lecture me. I know what you think of this whole thing already."

"Joce, you know I love you." She walks over and hugs me loosely to avoid wrinkling my clothes. "I just want you to be happy."

"I am happy. If this didn't satisfy me, I wouldn't do it."

She sighs, nodding as she pulls away. Arguing with me is useless, she knows that, but I do love that she tries anyway.

"I can't believe you've accepted an invitation to go out!"

I turn to leave, rolling my eyes at her. "He gave me a ride and asked me. I saw how he looked at me; turning him down would've been stupid."

She follows me as I exit, her excitement making me wish I hadn't told her anything beyond the usual.

Dexter stands by the front door. As I approach, he holds out my jacket. "You want a ride?"

"Not really, but you'll insist anyway." I laugh, take the garment and slip my arms through, the lightness perfect for the weather tonight. "So let's go."

He winks and heads outside to the car, while I face Iris, who pulls me into a tight hug this time. "I want to hear all about it tomorrow!"

Another laugh as she releases me. "You know I'll tell you as much as I usually do."

She pouts, crossing her arms and making puppy dog eyes at me. This only lasts for a second before her phone rings and her eyes light up as she takes in the name on the screen. I know who it is: her boyfriend, Garret. She waves at me before answering and walks away.

When I reach the car, Dexter is waiting. He turns down the blaring music as I get in.

Dexter is a lot like Iris. While he's a man who loves sex, he actually prefers relationships. He has also elected himself my brother, saying since I don't have one, that someone has to look out for me. And by look out, he means lecture me every chance he gets to try and persuade me to change my ways.

Like right now, not even one second after he pulls away from the curb. "You know I wish you wouldn't do this. You never know what could happen."

I give him the 'are you kidding me?' look, but he's focused on the road. "By that logic, I shouldn't drive a car. Or even go outside my house without someone with me.

Or hell, stay inside my house because someone could break in. See how ridiculous this is?"

"Yeah, but it's worse. Because—"

"No." I scowl at him as we approach the hotel. "I'll be fine. I've given both of you his name just in case, but everything will be fine, and you know it."

I don't see what I do as reckless; after all, I have Iris and Dexter, a system to let them know how it is going at specific intervals...and a thing of mace.

Even so, I refuse to live in fear. Life is an adventure, one I will always live to the fullest.

He frowns back at me after we arrive, so I lean over and give him a hug. He squeezes once before releasing me and I grin at him, feeling grateful and playful.

"Smile. I don't want the last thing I see before dying to be your frown."

He grips the steering wheel and throws me a disgusted look. "That's not funny!"

I roll my eyes and open the door, chuckling. "Later, Dex. Love ya."

He laughs while I'm stepping out of the vehicle and after shutting the door, I head into the hotel to wait for what I hope will be the best sex of my life.

CHAPTER THREE

The man really seems to like his suits.

Approaching the private table in the back where Tobias sits waiting for me, he stands up, and I instantly focus on his attire.

I've never been one to drool over a man in a suit or uniform, yet this time I am unable to stop myself from staring as he pulls out my chair.

He's changed into a black one for dinner. He wears no vest — only a white shirt, no ties, with the first button undone. His hair is rather tame if a bit unruly and all I want to do is run my hands through it. I don't know why he changed his clothes, but I certainly don't mind the more relaxed air he's giving off.

When he lifts a brow at my inspection, I merely smile and sit down.

"Thank you."

"You're welcome." He grins and takes a seat across from me.

The waiter comes and takes our drink order. Then we're left alone.

"I trust you had a nice day?" His voice is pleasant and low.

"I did. And you?"

"Yes." He sits forward, all his intense attention focused on me, and the tension between us escalates. "You are stunning."

I want to suck in a breath at the blatant desire shining from his eyes, but manage to control the impulse. Barely.

The waiter arrives before I can respond and sets our drinks down. "Are you ready to order?"

Tobias nods and looks at me.

"Yes." I don't look at the menu, giving the waiter a smile because he knows me well at this point, since I tend to order the same thing every visit here. "May I please get the six-ounce filet, medium-rare, with a loaded baked potato? That's all."

He writes it down as I look back at Tobias. He smirks at me as the waiter turns to him.

"I'll have the same."

"Very good. I'll put this right in for you, Mr. Blackburn."

He takes our menus and rushes off while Tobias grins, taking a drink of his water.

"Do you always copy what your date orders?" I take a sip of my own water, making sure to keep my face neutral. "First, the water. Then, the steak and potato."

He shrugs. "I do when they order the same things I like."

I want to smile because I really like him. If I were the type of girl to have relationships, he would be at the top of my list. Smart, funny, sexy, educated, and obviously doing well for himself. A girl could do much worse.

Instead, my self-preservation kicks in, the mere idea of a long-term relationship crossing my mind raising my hackles. "The waiter knows you by name. You must come here often."

"Funny. I thought the same thing when I told the host a woman named Luna would be joining me, and he knew exactly to whom I referred."

I don't blush like I'm sure he expects me to, laughing and lifting my glass of water instead. "Touché!"

"You're a fascinating woman, Luna." He touches his glass to mine, then takes a sip before continuing. "I've seen you inside here a fair bit."

On the outside, I keep my face calm; on the inside, I panic, because it makes me question how much he knows about me. "Have you? And what have you seen, exactly?"

"A woman who isn't finding what she desires." He meets my eyes directly, confident in the sexy, alpha kind of way. "A problem I think I can help with."

The panic subsides a bit as my curiosity takes over. "And what do you think I desire that I'm not finding?"

His eyes spark, and he holds his hand out, palm up. I don't know what instinct takes over, but I do know what he wants. Placing my hand in his, my breath hitches as a wave of awareness rolls through me at his touch. Maybe the response is because I want him to put his hands all over me; I can't really be sure.

A tug on my hand has me leaning in, closing the distance between our faces over the table. He turns my hand over and brings his lips to kiss the center of it. The brief touch arouses me, heightened by the accompanying lick, making me wish we were alone right this fucking instant.

Then his tongue travels down, leaving a trail of kisses and licks to my fingertips before he takes my middle finger into his mouth, sucking on it. His eyes are locked on mine, somehow preventing me from looking away, and I bite my lip to stifle a moan.

I cross my legs, trying to drag my hand away at the sound of footsteps approaching, except he has all the power. Swirling his tongue around it one more time before sucking hard, he releases his hold on me. We both barely sit back before the waiter rounds the corner, our food in hand.

After a moment, we are alone with our dinner, and as I

pick up my silverware, Tobias finally answers my question with one word.

"Me."

I glance up, unable to speak at the hungry look in his eyes, his lips curving into a smile as I freeze. There's little doubt he knows how incredibly turned on I am as he clarifies, even though it's unnecessary.

"I'm what you desire. And after dinner, I'll prove it to you."

I swallow, my mouth dry, even as I nod.

This night will be an interesting one and I can't wait.

❦

"I've gotten a room for the evening." Tobias pulls out the key as we head to the elevators. "I thought you'd feel safer here."

I mentally add 'considerate' to his ever-growing list of qualities, but that doesn't prevent me from messing with him.

When I stop dead in my tracks, the arm he has around my waist slides out since he didn't anticipate my sudden pause, causing him to turn around with a questioning look.

"Is there a problem?"

"I never said we were going to sleep together." My eyes are focused on the floor to give off the impression I'm embarrassed by this turn of events. "I thought we were just having dinner."

He doesn't say anything and after a few moments, I glance up to find him grinning.

"I didn't say we were going to either, did I?" He walks over to the elevator and presses the 'up' icon, then holds out his hand. "Are you coming or not?"

Well, that didn't go like I thought it would. Interesting. Perhaps this man knows as much about playing the game as I do.

Taking his hand, we get on the elevator, where he presses the top floor button as the doors close.

Neither of us speaks, the quietness unnerving. This evening feels different from the others. I can't decipher his intentions and that leaves me on edge because I always know what to expect from beginning to end.

His comment at dinner about proving I desire him seemed to indicate we would be partaking in sexual activities.

I haven't misunderstood, have I? Perhaps he intends to tease me all night?

I'm lost in thought when he chuckles. "Did you just growl?"

My face flushes. "I—I guess so."

Did I seriously just stutter? What is wrong with me?

I lift my eyes to meet his as he snickers. He's staring down at me, eyes intent and desirous, seconds before he pushes me until my back is against the wall. A hand slides down my side and lifts up my leg to wrap it around his hip. He steps closer, pinning me to the wall, as his lips descend on mine.

Eager for this since his little stunt at dinner, I open my mouth intuitively, giving him immediate access as my eyes drift shut. His tongue seeks out mine as my hands land on his shoulders, where I slide them up into his sleek hair, and indulge my earlier desire to run my fingers through his hair as our mouths mingle.

The hand holding my leg skims back toward my skirt, then under it. I'm not wearing hose, and when he cups me over the silk panties I donned, we both moan. Bucking into his hand, it's impossible to ignore the way his other hand tightens on my hip as the one cupping my pussy slides back and forth, providing me with the very sensations I want at that moment.

I barely register the dinging of the elevator as it continues the trek upward, fully engulfed in the tightening spiral of arousal shooting through me. I move my lower body again, grinding and trying to increase the pleasure, but I'm completely trapped. He seems perfectly content to ravage my mouth while stroking me at a leisurely, torturous pace.

He releases my mouth, murmuring his command against the corner of my lips. "Open your eyes."

I obey his command, gasping as he brings one hand up

to grip my chin, making sure I'm unable to look away. The hand stroking me through the silky material drifts up to the band, then slips inside and down to my slick folds. His eyes hold mine captive as he inserts a finger inside me, then two, thrusting upward and making me cry out. His thumb finds my clit, rubbing it as his fingers curl inside me, massaging my g-spot.

His eyes burn as he pushes against me, arousal evident.

I want him inside me as much, if not more, than he wants the same thing.

Eager to get back to the room, my eyes dart to look at what level we're on.

Forty-four. Six more.

Dammit.

"Luna."

I bring my focus back to him. He smiles as he inserts another finger and I stiffen as the pleasure heightens again. I'm close, the orgasm just out of my reach, and he knows it.

Ding!

He moves his hand faster, and I move in rhythm. He leans in, kissing down my jaw, as his hand manipulates me.

Ding!

Then, his hand is gone. He slides my body down, leaving me on the edge of desire, and I wobble as he goes to move away.

"Here, let me help." He picks me up as if I weigh

nothing and tosses me over his shoulder as the elevator dings one last time. "We've arrived."

It stops, and I look over my shoulder, eyes flying to the monitor.

Forty-seven.

Tobias steps out into the hallway, chuckling. "Thought we were going to level fifty, didn't you?"

"I—" I lick my lips. "I saw you hit fifty!"

"I did, but you were a little too preoccupied with my one hand to notice I did anything else."

He's left me hanging on purpose! "Jackass."

As he stops in front of a door and runs the key through the reader, his laughter is completely playful. "A little anticipation never hurt anyone."

He opens the door and steps through, the door shutting softly behind us.

I can't stop the shiver of excitement that rushes through me at knowing the time has come to finally get what I came here for tonight.

CHAPTER FOUR

AFTER HE SETS ME DOWN INSIDE THE ROOM, I WALK toward the wide expanse of windows on the outer wall, giving me a view of the entire city.

Tobias walks up behind me after a few moments and places his hands on my shoulders.

"I've never been above floor forty," I muse out loud. "It's crazy how the view is so much better."

He rests his chin on my shoulder, looking out with me, as his fingertips skim up and down my arms.

"I came to the city ten years ago for college." His words are soft and he plants a kiss on the nape of my neck, causing a delicious shiver to run down my spine. "I've found that whether you're on the top level of a fifty-floor hotel, in the street below surrounded by buildings and people, or lying on your back in the middle of a grassy field staring up at the stars, the view is always stunning. Makes you realize how small you are in comparison to everything else, no matter your size."

At that, I turn in his arms, intrigued by what he said and he straightens, gliding his hands up to my waist before resting them there.

He's tall enough I have to lift my head a little to look straight into his desire-filled eyes, but not much. He's roughly six inches taller than me, so a nice six-two with a body that can pin me to an elevator wall without him breaking a sweat.

"I'd've never pegged you for a country boy." I'm teasing him, which is not something I normally do with men I'm trying to sleep with, and when he grins, I wrap my arms around his neck. "Ten years. That would make you twenty-eight?"

I don't know why I am asking questions. I'm interested in having sex with him and nothing else.

Perhaps because he doesn't seem very eager to get me in bed right away. He seems like the slow and steady type; the kind that likes to take their time and worship their lover's body.

I certainly will not complain in that case. Nothing better than a lover who takes their time and makes sure I'm as satisfied as they are by the end.

"Close. I'm thirty." His smile widens. "I didn't go to kindergarten until I was six. Then I took a year break after high school."

I almost ask why he took a year off when his hands roam my upper body, slide beneath the edge of my shirt to rest on my bare skin, and makes me forget about everything except this moment. He strokes just under my ribcage with his thumb on either side, then gives a tender squeeze before moving them up. One arm enfolds me in his hold, snug against his body as the other continues its trek upward until his palm's cupping a lace-encased breast.

My breath hitches as he holds my gaze. I barely blink before he's unhooked my bra and cups me again. His thumb rubs back and forth over my nipple, which tightens and rises immediately; he moves to the other side and repeats.

When I tug his head down and press my lips against his, he lifts me off the ground. My legs wrap around his waist, the action instinctive, and he carries me over to the bed.

I hum into his mouth when he grips my ass, frantic for us to be skin-to-skin already, and lower my legs to the floor.

Our lips are still fused as I shove my hands under his suit jacket to push it down his arms. He helps me, shrugging it off and then grabs the hem of my shirt, yanking it up and over my head. I slide the straps of my bra down my arms as he watches with hooded eyes.

After the garment drops to the floor, it's a race to become undressed. Buttons fly, shoes land across the room, and before long we are standing naked inches apart from each other.

I kneel, relishing the sudden intake of his breath as I take his cock in my palm and squeeze.

He grips my hair with a gentle tug, forcing me to look up at him and I lick my lips while glancing back down, he practically growls his next words.

"Damn woman, are you going to stare at it like a lollipop, or are you going to put me in your mouth?"

I laugh, delighted at having him at my mercy, waiting for me to give him what he wants. "Either way, I'll be sucking you like you're my favorite treat."

He inhales sharply as I put the head of his cock in my mouth. Using the tip of my tongue, I give him short, quick licks on the crown, followed by languid, leisurely licks on the underside of the head. His hand flexes in my hair, the rest of his body taut with self-restraint, as I lick him down the shaft and back up.

I repeat the action a few times before I cup his balls in my free hand and use the other to squeeze the shaft, finally sucking on it like I know he wants me to.

"Ah, fuck." Holding my head motionless, he thrusts once, then twice before pulling out of my mouth and smiling. "As much as I'd love to come in that pretty little mouth of yours, I want you to bend over the edge of the bed. Now."

His words arouse me to the point of desperation.

This is exactly what I've been waiting for. I didn't mind him being sweet earlier because I knew once we got down to business, his dominant nature would rear its head.

He can't help it...and its what I need, more than anything else this second. Dropping my gaze to the ground, I immediately obey, scrambling over to the bed.

Leaning over, I use my elbows to prop myself up, not daring to look behind me. Not even when the silence drags long enough to make me wonder what he's doing.

Then, he grips my thighs, his lips bestowing kisses along the curve of my backside. He uses his hands to push my legs apart gently, indicating I should widen my stance, which I do. His fingers start to move. He massages my legs, pressing his fingers in and making me moan as his lips and tongue move closer to my pussy. I lift my hips, begging him silently to put his mouth there, and lower my head to the bed.

He laughs, the sound wicked and delightful all in one. He parts me with one hand, inserts a finger from the other, and gives me exactly what I want.

The first lick is almost an overload since I am turned on enough I might come any minute. Clenching around his finger and tongue, the vibration from his chuckle is evident as he inserts another digit. His pace is unhurried, the two fingers stroking my g-spot as his tongue laps up the arousal his attention is coaxing from my body.

"Oh, god," I sob as he moves to my clit and licks at the

same undemanding pace despite my desire for more. "Please..."

I can't even articulate what I'm begging for, but he knows. I rock into his touch as he takes it into his mouth and sucks. Between that delectable torture and his fingers, I'm incoherent, the tension inside my body rising until my orgasm rips through me, stealing my breath.

Then, he's gone. I barely register the sound of foil tearing before his hands are back on my hips, his cock sinking into me from behind with one smooth thrust.

He pauses, his moan of pleasure mingling with mine as he covers my body with his. Placing his palm flat on the front of my neck, he lifts my head up and tilts it back until his mouth is right next to my ear. The hand clutching my hip tightens as he rocks our bodies together again before going still.

"You're fucking exquisite," he whispers, running his tongue from the lobe of my ear up to the top before continuing with dirty talk I can't help except love. "I think you should know that you have the most beautiful cunt I've ever seen or tasted."

"I wouldn't know, I can't see it from up here." The jokes is lost among the gasp escaping when his grip tightens on my neck, exposing more of the sensitive skin to the scrape of his teeth. "But you feel so damned good. If you don't keep going, I'll have to find a way to finish the job myself."

"So demanding." He pulls out almost completely before plunging back in and mutters against my neck, "I can see that next time I'll have to bring something extra to occupy that mouth of yours so you can't speak."

He pulls out and flips me over, capturing my lips with his own and thrusting his tongue into my mouth before I can tell him there won't be a next time. Whimpering into his mouth as he reconnects our bodies, I wrap my legs around his hips. He starts with a gentle in and out, then speeds up, our mouths warring in pace with the pounding of his cock.

Tearing his lips away, he brings up a hand and presses it lightly around my neck, thumb caressing where my pulse throbs. "Is this okay?"

I nod, finding myself trusting him to do it properly even though I don't know him that well.

His hand tightens a little more as a sob of excitement escapes my throat. "Are you good?"

The pleasure flooding through me clouds my brain, but I know he's asking if he's good to finish. I close my eyes and smile, inclining my head to indicate 'yes'. He thrusts to the hilt once, then twice, and stiffens, his hand automatically releasing its hold on my neck as he rests atop me.

Nothing is said for a few moments, the only sounds in the room our heavy breathing, and when he finally rolls off me, that's when the familiar panic sets in.

I knew this would happen one day, that I would feel a

connection to someone I had sex with. No awkwardness, no fumbling between us. Just straight up pure and amazing sex with a partner who gives me what I need intuitively.

I just hadn't expected to experience that with him.

Fuck, fuck, fuck!

Needing to escape *now*, I jump up and start gathering my clothes.

"What are you doing?"

"I—I need to leave." Shoving my shirt on, I glance around the floor for my underwear. Not seeing them, I slip on the skirt and hope it's not too breezy on the walk home. "I'm sorry."

Turning toward him, I hop on one foot to put my heels on and try not to the way my insides are tumbling show on my face.

"Why?" He shoves a hand through his hair and stands. "What's wrong?"

His confusion is written all over his face, but I can't explain. He won't get it. His own words from earlier indicated he thought this might end up being something more.

I can't let that happen; I have to shut him down before the idea can grow into something I'm suddenly feeling like I might not say no to now. What the hell?

"Thanks for the fuck." My cheerfulness is forced as his face clouds, irritation at my choice of words combining with the puzzlement at my behavior. "But I've really gotta run now."

I look away, unable to stand the unexpected guilt that fills me. Grabbing my phone and purse from the floor, I head toward the door.

"Luna!"

I expect him to come running after me, yet when I look over my shoulder, he's just standing there, grinning.

"This isn't over, Luna," he promises. "I will see you later."

"No." I shake my head because there's no way that will happen if I can avoid it. "No, you won't."

And while exiting the room, I realize my days of being Luna have officially come to an end.

My friends will be thrilled.

CHAPTER FIVE

I'T'S WEDNESDAY MORNING, AND I'M HIDING IN THE office, head down on the desk when Molly walks in. "Are you all right?"

Shaking my head without lifting it, the papers under my arm shuffle, and she sighs.

Approaching me, she places a comforting hand on my shoulder. "It'll work out. There has to be something that can be done."

Her words are so filled with hope and faith in things working out which only makes tears well in my eyes because if this place goes under, I'm not the only person losing my job.

"There isn't." Looking up at her, one tear slides down my cheek and I wipe it away, sniffling. "I'm sorry, Molly. I —I've tried s-so hard this past year to b-bring us out of debt, b-but..."

As I trail off, trying not to sob, she frowns. "It's not your fault. At least you tried, right? And—"

The ding of the door interrupts our conversation, and I glance at the clock, only to widen my eyes at the time.

"Oh god." I swipe at my eyes, knowing I look like shit because I've been crying on and off since five this morning. "It's h-him. I c-can't let him see me like this."

"You know he'll ask for you anyway."

I groan and cover my face. "Yes, I know. Tell him that I'm sorry, but I am busy with other things."

"Like that'll work," she mutters, taking a step back. "But I'll give it a shot."

She leaves the office, and I stare at the letter from my bank. Truth is, there's no way I'm not going to lose my diner.

I inherited it a year ago, not long after I graduated college when my father died unexpectedly, and what a disaster he left behind for me.

Discovering how much trouble he'd been having devastated me, adding anger to my grief. The bills were piling up, the diner wasn't making money, and my father had been quite late on several loan payments over the previous year.

In an attempt to keep the diner in the family, I've been working my ass off. Decisions were made to scale down portions, make the menu smaller, and keep the staff hired to a minimum.

But the reality is, I still haven't gotten ahead. Any profit made has gone straight to fixing things around the diner, especially those that have to meet standards and stay up-to-code. Then, last month, business dropped to a point I've had to scrape everything I could find together, which resulted in a late payment on the loan.

Even though that had been the first late payment in over a year, the bank has obviously had enough.

They are calling the loan in, wanting their money in the near future, and I don't have it.

My lawyer, whom I also owe money to, said my only option is to find a private lender willing to take on the debt.

So far, we haven't managed to find one inclined to take on a business in such dire straits.

When the door opens, I lift my eyes from the paper, expecting to see Molly only to find Tobias standing in the doorway. His worried face, along with the unexpected and unwelcome surge of arousal at the sight of him, ignites the anger I've been holding back at this whole situation.

"What are you doing back here?" I slam the paper down on my desk and reach for a tissue, dabbing at my eyes. "This is an employee-only area."

He doesn't say anything as he walks closer and sits down in the seat across from me.

Tossing the used tissue in the trash, I stand up and point at the door, my voice rising. "Didn't you hear me? Get out!"

He sits back and crosses his arms, ignoring my command completely. "Why are you crying?"

Realizing he's not going to leave as asked, I sit down and mimic his pose. Lifting a brow, I ignore his question and question him instead. "How did you get back here?"

"I walked."

I glare at him.

"Okay, okay!" He puts his hands up in the air in a mock surrender. "I ordered food after that waitress — what's her name? Oh right, Molly! Anyway, I did order breakfast after Molly told me you were truly busy with other things. But when she went into the kitchen, I heard her say to the cook that you were upset—"

"You were spying."

"No—"

"Please." Wiping my nose with another tissue, I stare at him, my anger evident through my tone. "You would've had to stand up and get close to the counter to hear such a thing unless you weren't sitting at your usual table. Therefore, you were being nosy."

He grins and leans in, eyes softening. "Okay, I'm busted. But she looked upset as well, and I was curious, so when she wasn't looking I came back here to find you. Now, tell me what's going on."

I hesitate, not even wanting him here. What if he finds out I'm Luna, the woman he screwed not even forty-eight hours ago? The same one who walked out right after in a

43

big fucking hurry and promised he would never see her again?

Problem is, I don't know anyone else and am running out of options. Which is why I pick up the paper and hold it out to him, even though the chance he can help is highly unlikely.

"I'm not sure why you even care—"

He cuts me off with an angry glare of his own as he takes the letter from my hand. "I come in here three times a week and demand that you are the one to serve me. Think about that while I read this."

I open my mouth only to shut it without retorting as he scans the paper. Funny how I never questioned his insistence on having me serve him, merely considering it the quirk of a customer.

My thought about what he means when he says to think about it is interrupted as his eyes widen, flying up to meet mine once more as his lips twist.

"This is pretty fucking bad, Ms. Bates." He puts the letter down and stabs the paper with his finger. "How the fuck did it get to this point?"

Even though I swear myself, his emphasis on the word fuck makes me wince because I'm screwed, for certain. I don't need him to tell me this, but his accusatory tone without knowing all the facts pisses me right off.

"Fuck you." I point a finger at him and then at the

door. "You don't know anything about what I've been dealing with, so you can go on and get the fuck out."

He doesn't move and the door flies open.

"Jocelyn, that man—" Molly stumbles inside only to stop short, eyes wide at the sight of Tobias sitting in the chair. "Oh, I'm sorry! I didn't know—"

He stands up and holds out his hand, grinning. "You may call me Tobias."

Her face flushes and suddenly, I'm irritated at both of them. "Molly, you're fine. Mr. Giles-Blackburn here was just leaving, weren't you?"

"I believe we still have some business to attend to." He sits back down, then tosses Molly another smile. "Would you bring me something to drink, please?"

When she opens her mouth to object, I cut in. "Please go take care of things up front, Molly. He doesn't need a drink because he won't be here long enough to need one."

She looks from him to me and back again, then tosses him an apologetic glance before exiting the room. As she closes the door behind her, he chuckles.

"I don't know what's so amusing."

"Oh, nothing." He relaxes in the chair once more. "I was asking myself how you knew my last name. Then I realized you would've seen it on my credit card when I pay."

When I remain quiet, he taps the letter from the bank.

"If you will accept my assistance, I may be able to help solve your problem."

Utter disbelief causes me to roll my eyes. "Unless you know a private lender willing to lend money to a person who is barely scraping by, I highly doubt you can."

"I do." He pulls out a card and a pen from his pocket, writing on the back before holding it out to me. "Come to this address tonight at eight and bring any documents pertaining to this diner, including the menu and your inventory."

I take the card as he rises and addresses me with an indiscernible look. "Any questions?"

"This—this looks like a private address."

"It is. It's mine."

What? Does this mean he's the private lender who is going to give me the money I need to save the diner? Unbelievable. And to invite me to his house, of all places, to talk about this... what will he want for his help?

Nothing is free, after all.

He winks at me when I don't respond to what he's said. "Don't be late."

With that, he turns on his heel and departs, shutting the door softly behind him.

Leaving me with the feeling that the very person who might be able to save my diner may end up being the one person whose help I have to turn down, no matter the consequences.

CHAPTER SIX

TOBIAS DOESN'T ANSWER THE DOOR RIGHT AWAY WHEN I ring the bell and the longer he makes me wait, the more I want to leave without hearing what he has to offer.

I wouldn't mind if it weren't for the fact I'm five minutes late, standing on a porch in a strange neighborhood where everything is pitch black except the dimly lit street lights.

And the longer I stand here in front of a gorgeous house leaving me to only guess at the amount of his wealth, the more nervous I am.

Iris and Dexter know I'm at his place; I gave them his address just in case. Both were adamant about me letting Tobias assist me with saving the diner, if he can. They have no idea why I want to say no, even though they are both aware he's the same man I slept with on Monday.

When I informed them I would no longer be going out

as Luna, Dexter's relief had been so palatable he picked me up and twirled me around. Iris waited until later that evening to question me, seeming skeptical when I told her that it no longer makes me happy so I'm done with it.

She knows me too well.

The door opening jerks me from my thoughts, only to discover Tobias standing in front of me wearing jeans and nothing else.

I should've bolted, but it's too late now.

"Jocelyn." He steps aside to indicate I should enter, his grin unrepentant. "I can call you Jocelyn at this point, yes?"

I nod, stepping over the threshold and pausing as he shuts the door, clasping my hands in front of me.

"This way."

He walks away, and I follow his lead.

Staring at his ass the whole way, I relive every moment of the other night — from his mouth and lips on my pussy to his cock pounding into me with stamina I know many men could only hope they possessed. And the exquisite way his hand felt around my throat?

Fuck.

I can't help it. It's been nearly two days, and going without sex even this long is frustrating.

As we enter a room, I glance around, quickly establishing that we're in what must be his office.

"Please, take a seat."

Sinking into the soft, cloth-covered chair in front of the desk, I cross my legs and clear my throat nervously.

Taking a seat behind the desk, he places his hand out, palm up.

Gathering that he wants the papers, I hand them over.

"Thank you. Give me just a few moments to look over these."

I nod, but he's no longer looking at me. Figuring he knows how attractive he is to women, I openly gawk while he shuffles through the documents.

He's freshly showered, his glistening hair still damp. His mouth is pursed a bit as he concentrates. When he licks a finger, then uses it to flip to a new page like in a book, I am strangely turned on.

My thighs clench together involuntarily, already intimately aware of what this man can provide when given the chance.

I close my eyes, wishing I could touch myself at this moment as I imagine him glancing up, discovering my eyes on him. He smiles and stands up, coming around to stand behind me. He slides his hands down and into my shirt, cupping my breasts in his hands and squeezing my nipples, making me moan. Kissing up and down my neck, he fondles me inside my top as I lift my arms up and shove my hands through his hair. I tug on it a bit, and he hisses, paying me back with a soft bite on my neck that heightens my arousal tenfold.

With a chuckle, he uses one hand to go even further south, unbuttoning my jeans and sliding down the zipper before slipping inside. Soon, he's fingering me, his thumb manipulating my clit and I'm so wet, so turned on that it will only take a few minutes before I'm shaking with the force of my orgasm.

I moan, wanting his cock inside me as his hand slips away, and he asks, "Are you going to be sick or something?"

Huh?

"Ms. Bates!"

At his shout, I force my eyes open, cheeks flushing at the concerned look on his face and mortified at allowing myself to fantasize to that point in his presence.

"Ah..." I swallow, giving him a weak smile. Does he know what I was thinking? I hope not. "Sorry. I was lost in thought."

He stares at me, and I resist the urge to look away. Finally, he stands up and comes around to sit on the edge of his desk, mouth set in a grim line.

"I had no idea your father was having such a bad time. I would've helped him."

I start at the mention of my father, my eyes rounding in surprise. "You knew my father?"

"I've been going to the diner three mornings a week for years. Your father was a kind man."

"Years?" That doesn't make sense. "How so? I didn't see you there until six months after I took over."

He sighs and clears his throat. "Your father was like my dad away from home. We spent a lot of time together when I wasn't busy. Right before he died, we went fishing." He gets up and walks over to the window and stares out. "He had a lot of regrets, including his daughter whom he said he hadn't seen in years."

My stomach drops, my lungs suddenly incapable of supporting my breathing. I clutch the arms of my chair, but he doesn't notice since he's faced away.

"He talked about her all the time. Every single time we went fishing, she was on his mind. I asked him once, after a year of those trips, what she looked like. 'Raven black hair with eyes that are sometimes grey and at other times blue, but with the face of an angel,' unlike him. He was full of pride, never saying a bad word about her, talking about how she was off at college and would be the first in the family to graduate. So, on our last fishing trip, I finally asked him, what's her name?"

Tobias turns around, his eyes blazing with desire as they land on me. "He said, 'Her name is Jocelyn, but ever since she was a little girl, she's always been my Luna.'"

Of course. I knew before he reached the last line that he knows who I am and has since he pulled over on the curb that day.

Jumping up, I run for the door, even though he'll catch me.

And he does, because he's quick on his feet. Twirling

me around, he traps me between his body and the wall. His grasp is gentle as he takes my chin in hand, eyes glinting with lust as he grins at me.

I'm not afraid even if this man holds all the cards right now to my future. His touch tells me he'll never hurt me, at least physically.

He bends his head, pressing our lips together for just a moment, then withdraws enough to whisper against my lips.

"Game's over, Luna. I win."

I smile and close my eyes, bringing his mouth back to mine, knowing he has no idea at all that the game isn't over.

It's just getting started.

CHAPTER SEVEN

~Present~

I DON'T KNOW WHAT'S REAL ANYMORE.

The room is filled with people chattering. Someone is styling my hair while another does my nails while I silently sit here mulling the options available to me.

Panic and run is at the top of the list.

I should stand up, announce my mistake in thinking I could do this, express how sorry I am, and then make a dash for the exit.

But I can't.

No. I *won't*, because I don't break promises and agreed to an entire year. I won't back out now; losing everything that matters to me is the last thing I want.

One year isn't that long, after all.

At least, that's what I keep telling myself.

I just hope nothing else is lost in the process.

Like my heart...

Or my life.

Three Weeks Before...

TOBIAS' LIPS DEVOUR MINE.

He caught me when I ran after revealing he's known about my disguise all along. I kissed him after his victory to avoid telling him something better left unsaid.

And in this moment, I want this to continue. I need his touch so badly it hurts.

Two days since we fucked and I ache for more as never before. Between the kissing now and the memories of the sex we had, my body is on fire.

Is it sex in general I want, or sex with him specifically? I'm pissed the answer isn't more clear. Either way, I'm screwed and not in the way I like.

Pulling my mouth away from his, I turn my face to the side, needing to take a breath and think about what the hell to say now.

I suppose he thinks I'm only taking a short break because he starts kissing down the side of my neck and rocks into me, making his desire quite clear. What he needs right this second is me and although part of me wishes I could give that to him, as well as take what I want and need… I can't.

Sleeping with a person more than once is not something I've ever done, and even though my nights out as Luna are finished, I don't think changing my rules now is smart, not even for him.

No. Scratch that. *Especially* for him.

"I can't do this." Whispering, I push against his chest a little with the palms of my hands, but the action isn't convincing. "Let me go."

He stops long enough to ask, "Can't?" Then, he gives my neck a quick lick that causes a shiver to run through me before he inquires, "Or won't?"

"Both, damn you."

Thankfully, I don't have to repeat my request for him to let me go. He backs off, releasing me from my imprisonment against the wall even as his hands grip my upper arms.

"Steady?" I nod, and he removes his hands, turning back toward the study, his entire manner growing aloof. "I believe we still have business to discuss."

A few moments after he walks off, I follow him, and he's sitting behind his desk when I enter, staring at me as I take a seat.

"Tell me why I should help you." He pulls a file filled with papers out of a drawer. "You said the diner was your fathers' business, but I learned you and him hadn't spoken in years before he died. Why is that?"

I curl my hands into fists. How is it possible for a man who almost had me begging him to fuck me moments ago to piss me off so quickly with one question?

"The issues I had with my father are none of your concern." I point at the documents on his desk. "You saw the trouble my father was in before I got here. Things have improved immensely since I took over. The problem is all the money he owed before his death has been eating what little profit I am making."

"Fair enough." He nods and leans forward, clasping his hands together as he frowns. "Here's the thing, though. You need more money than someone just taking over this loan for you, if you wish to ever make a profit."

My stomach drops even as I keep the worry from showing on my face. I've feared hearing someone say that even though I've done the best I can, but my troubles have always been more than I can possibly handle by myself.

"You will have trouble finding any lender who will buy out your loan, let alone give you enough extra money to pay all these collectors. Not with the way these documents show continual losses." He sits back and folds his arms. "How have you been paying your personal bills? You can barely pay what little staff you have."

I hate his questions, but he did say he might be able to help me, so I need to tell him what he wants to know. Even so, I count in my head to three, mainly to swallow back any possible attitude that might try to make its way out, and then answer.

"I live with my two friends. They pay the bills, as they know how much I'v been struggling recently. They don't want me to lose the diner any more than I do."

As he watches me while not saying anything, I resist the urge to squirm...and, strangely, the urge to babble.

Finally, he grins, leaning back in his chair with his hands behind his head. "I will help you."

I start to smile, only for that small glimmer of hope to sink when he adds, "On one condition."

I'm not sure what that condition will be, but something tells me I am not going to like it and scowl at him. "And what would that be?"

"First, the terms I'm offering are in this file." He straightens and hands the folder to me. "Once you and your lawyer go over them and you agree to my conditions, I will sign them."

I open the file to glance at the documents as he continues, "I will pay the loan off for you. You will also receive enough money to pay off all the past due bills and fix or replace anything that needs done." I look up and gape at him after reading the large sum on the papers. "That includes the money you owe the lawyer."

"You..." I clear my throat, tearing filling my eyes, and

slam the folder shut. "You already knew how much I trouble I was in."

He runs his hand through his hair, his eyes never leaving mine. "It's my business to know these things. Anybody with half a brain could see you were struggling. I didn't know how much until my lawyer met with yours. However, I had no idea it started with your father and has been going on for a while."

I don't even know what to say. I had given the lawyer my permission to discuss the details with anyone who might be able to help, so I can't even be mad that this man has known the details of my situation for quite some time, apparently.

Dropping my eyes from his to stare down at the papers, I force myself to accept I'm going to have to take his help no matter the cost and ask the question I really need to know the answer to. "What is the condition?"

I wait for his answer for what seems like an eternity, only for him to laugh.

"Luna—Jocelyn—dammit, what do you prefer to be called?"

I actually love the sound of Luna on his lips. The way he says it has my body humming every time, but I don't want him to know that. I don't look up when answering him.

"Jocelyn is the better way to go. The last thing I need is

for anyone to figure out that I was Luna; it's bad enough you know."

"All right, Jocelyn. The condition is..." He pauses. Really drags the moment out, long enough I glance up at him to find him smiling at me with a mischievous glint in his eyes. "The condition is that you marry me."

CHAPTER EIGHT

Well, if his aim was to freak me out, he has succeeded.

I jump up from my chair. "Absolutely not!"

He doesn't seem shocked by my reaction, smiling and lifting a brow as if he hasn't just asked a woman he barely knows to marry him. "Do you have any other options?"

"You know I don't." Sighing, I sit back down and rub my temples. "Doesn't mean I am going to say yes to your offer."

He chuckles. "You would be insane not to accept, Jocelyn."

"Well, maybe I am insane!" Snapping at him, I place the papers on the edge of his desk before pointing a finger at him. "Or perhaps you are the certifiable one for even asking. You don't even know me. Hell, I barely know you."

"Won't getting married solve that issue rather quick?"

I throw my hands up in the air. "Why in the world do you want to marry me? What's wrong with doing this out of the kindness of your heart or something?"

"I'm a businessman." He grins, leaning forward with his hands clasped atop the desk. "The truth is, you're doing a great job with the diner and have been since you took over. You've been paying off the debts, little by little, but not fast enough. You simply need money to bring yourself out of the red all at once. But nothing is free, Jocelyn. Everything has a cost, and my money comes with a price."

I ignore his compliment, even as I fill with pleasure at his acknowledgement of all my hard work, sticking to the heart of the matter. "Isn't the fact I have to pay you back enough of a price?"

He shakes his head. "If you marry me, I pay all of this for you. You don't need to pay me back."

My mouth drops open in shock but recover fast, asking, "And if I don't marry you?"

"Then you find someone else to help you."

Bastard.

"You don't want me to marry you." My assurance here is with the hope he'll see helping me without tying us together in matrimony is the smarter thing to do. "I mean, I've never even had a boyfriend. I will not make a good wife."

Both statements are true, but what am I doing? Neither of those facts sounds as if I'm saying no; rather that I think he should truly consider what he's offering because I'm not sure how I'll save my business by turning him down.

Yes, I lost this battle before I even knew there was one. He has the upper hand, but that doesn't mean I have to give in easily, however.

He tilts his head to the side a little and smirks. "What do you think being a wife involves?"

"Things I never wanted to do. Didn't you hear me say I've never been in a relationship?"

"Yes." He pushes back from his desk and stands up. "I don't see why that would bother me. It merely means you have less bad habits to break."

What?

"Bad habits?"

As he walks around the desk, I quell the urge to stand up and escape. After all, he'll catch me fast like he did earlier this evening. Making his way over to my chair, he stands in front, his legs touching my knees. Then, he places his hands on either side of me as he squats down to put us at equal eye level with each other.

"Bad habits. And no previous relationship baggage, such as assholes continually breaking your trust and treating you like crap. Unless...?"

I shake my head at his unspoken question. There is no one else I have feelings for and never has been.

He cups my face in his palm, and the contact has me sucking in a breath at the wave of lust that shoots through me. "Then why haven't you had a relationship? Something must've happened."

"Nope." He runs the pad of his thumb over my lips, and I lick my lips before continuing. "I'm just a woman who loves sex and doesn't want the complications that come with another person's expectations."

"Interesting." He brings his lips to mine and brushes them together in a tease before pulling away. "Looks like you no longer get to avoid expectations any longer."

"You—" A bolt of pleasure as he takes his attentions to my neck with a lick that has me shuddering. "You could probably have any woman you want. W-why me?"

He keeps his mouth on my neck and one hand cupping my face as the other glides up my jean clad leg in a slow, deliberate tease.

"Let's see..." His skims his mouth up to kiss behind my ear. "You're intelligent and funny. I already know we're sexually compatible. I've no doubt that you will fulfill all my desires, in the bedroom and out."

He takes the lobe of my ear into his mouth and sucks on it, moving the hand higher on my leg until it rests at the top of my thigh. He uses his thumb to caress me on the outside of my jeans, and I do my damnedest to show no response.

He releases my ear with one final lick, chuckling. "You're stubborn, and I will enjoy every moment spent trying to win you over. Plus, you already know how much I value routine and how I take my coffee."

I smile in spite of my determination to not give in.

Having him so close to me makes me want to give in because I want him to touch me, and that can't happen. I need to get away. Even if I feel a pull to him, as if we've known each other forever, the fact is we don't really know each other at all. It doesn't matter that I know how he likes his coffee or that the sex has been amazing; he's asking me for something I'm not sure I can give.

"I need to go." I push on his shoulders, this time with enough force to show him how serious I am. "I have to think about this."

He doesn't argue as he stands up; he doesn't need to. He knows I'll say yes in the end. I don't have control, not really, yet he's willing to let me pretend I do by letting me go. For now.

Moving back behind the desk, he sits down as I rise and grab the papers from his desk. "How long do I have to answer you?"

"A week." He grins because giving me a week or not, he's won. "Also, be ready to go out tomorrow night at six-thirty. We're going on our second date."

I glare at him for a moment, then turn toward the door, not feeling the need to acknowledge his demand.

"Oh, and Jocelyn?" He calls out as I'm about to exit, so I pause, waiting. "Wear a skirt, please. No hose."

I almost turn around at those words to demand why he wants me to wear a skirt, but that would be a dumb question because the garment provides easy access.

Instead, I hold up a hand and flip him the bird before walking out to the sound of his laughter.

❦

"I can't believe you're going to marry him!"

Me, Iris, and Dexter have just finished breakfast. I sigh at Iris' statement because this conversation is happening way too fucking early for me, even though I'm normally up at this time.

The previous evening with Tobias is specifically to blame for my crankiness this morning.

Want to save your business? Become my wife!

Who the fuck does he think he is?

"I didn't say yes. There has to be another way."

I know there isn't another solution for my problem, but damn I wish there were. Tobias unnerves me, and that isn't a good sign. By marrying him, I'm in serious jeopardy of... well, losing my freedom, for one.

Fuck, when did I start to sound like such a commitment-phobe?

Dexter laughs. "The universe sure caught up with you, didn't it?"

"The universe can suck my imaginary dick."

His amusement escalates as I scowl at him. "It's not imaginary. Soon, you'll be married to one of your very own."

Don't laugh!

"Screw you." Picking up the closest thing — a potholder — I aim it in the direction of his head, unable to keep the smirk from my face. "And how do we go from you being worried about my outings as Luna, to practically gleeful at me marrying a near stranger?"

When I throw it, he ducks, laughing when it hits Iris instead.

"Hey!" She looks up from her perusal of the papers Tobias gave me and scowls. "Knock it off you two! It's almost like you truly are related."

"Anything is possible," I retort, irritated. "After all, I've never even been in a relationship and I'm getting married."

She rolls her eyes.

Dexter walks over and places his arm around my shoulders. "Look, no matter what, I want you safe. People used to arrange marriages all the time to better their situations and fortunes. You've said there is no other way to save the restaurant — that you've run out of options. This isn't the same thing as what you did as Luna."

"Maybe I should've charged them and I wouldn't be in this situation at all." He scowls at that — and truthfully, I never would've done such a thing — and I shrug his arm off of me while heading in the direction of my bedroom. "I've gotta get ready for work."

Iris gasps. "Wait! Come here!"

I turn around and walk over to the table, then look down at papers. "What?"

"Did you even bother to read these?"

She is grinning at me. For what, I don't know since smiling is the last thing I feel like doing.

"I glanced at them, but..."

Okay, not admitting that I'd been too busy trying to subdue my lust to really pay attention to the papers.

When I don't finish my sentence, she laughs. "This is a prenuptial agreement!"

"Wouldn't it say that at the top of the papers?"

She pulls a sheet out and holds it up. Sure enough, there at the top makes crystal clear what these papers are.

"Why didn't I see that?"

She cracks up. "He put it on the bottom, most likely on purpose. You never got through them all."

I sigh. "I'll have my lawyer look them over, but—"

Iris cuts me off, mouth set in a straight line. "You know it's only for a year, right?"

And just like that, I'm fuming.

I stomp out of the room like a petulant child, vowing to tell Tobias exactly what I think of him and his little deception when we get together this evening.

CHAPTER NINE

I'm wearing jeans when Tobias arrives for our date.

Of course, he's wearing a suit.

He doesn't even comment at my attire, looking me up and down before smirking. "Ready to go?"

Maybe he forgot? Well, I'm certainly not going to remind him of his request.

I smile, shutting the door behind me with a snap. "Yes, I am."

And just like that, we're on our way.

I don't wonder how he knew where I lived or which apartment was mine. My address had been in the papers I showed him.

But, where the hell are we going? Not that I'm going to ask. Something tells me the less I speak tonight, the better, and it's not long before we're pulling into his driveway.

"I thought we were going on a date?" I take off my seatbelt and glare at him, irritated at the uneasiness creeping in. "I could've driven myself over here."

He doesn't answer as he turns off the car, then gets out. I scramble to do the same as he completely ignores me and heads to the front door.

I want to consider this rude, but the sudden feeling he remembers exactly what he told me creeps in, and there's no doubt this little visit to his house is from me completely ignoring his directions.

Crap!

I run to catch up, closing the door behind me as he continues walking toward his office.

"I'll be right back." He tosses a look back at me over his shoulder. "Stay right there."

The humor in his voice confuses me. He doesn't appear mad. If anything, he's amused, practically gleeful at whatever he has planned next.

Nodding, I remain where I am as he enters his office, my heart beginning to pound to longer he's gone.

I should leave, but my feet won't move.

Two minutes pass.

Three.

Yep, I'm definitely in trouble.

When he finally comes back out of the office, I smile at him. He holds out a hand, and I take it. He interlaces our fingers, gripping my hand firmly as he leads the way upstairs.

He doesn't say anything as we reach the tops of the steps and turn to the right, entering a bedroom.

His, no doubt.

"Take a seat." He points at the edge of the bed while I gulp, unsure whether I want to know what he's got planned. "I'll be just a moment."

I stare at the huge bed against the wall. He turns to walk away, and I whisper, "Tobias?"

He pivots, his face expressionless except for a lifted eyebrow and a wicked gleam in his eyes. "Is there a problem?"

I swallow. "Um..."

It figures I'd struggle with what to say right at this moment when I need my words more than ever.

He grins, stepping close and sliding his right hand along my neck, cupping the nape of my neck as he commands my gaze with his own.

I am mesmerized.

It's terrible really. I've no idea what to do because I've never allowed things to get out of my control. And even though I've done all I can, researched and studied every other avenue possible to save the diner, he's truly my last option.

There's no running, but I'll put up a fight the whole way; screaming, if I have to.

"You're the most stubborn woman I've ever met." His lips get close to mine, making my body ache with his proximity even as my brain screams 'danger!' and to run away. "And intelligent enough to know what's coming."

He backs away without giving me anything, then points to the bed.

Shit.

I lift my chin in defiance. "Make me."

"Come? Oh, I will. Eventually." He starts to walk away once more, then throws me a look over his shoulder. "You've got one minute to do as I've asked — oh, and now I want you to come up with your own personal safe word, too."

Unable to resist the urge, I flip him off as he disappears into an adjoining room, then consider how I can possibly throw him off his game.

I thought challenging him was the way to go, but maybe I am wrong. He didn't take the bait when I said 'make me', and nothing I do seems to ruffle his feathers in the slightest.

Seems being obedient to the extreme may be the way to go.

With that decision made, I strip off all my clothing and sit on the edge of the bed, crossing my legs and placing my hands over top one another on my knee.

Stepping back into the room, he pauses when his gaze falls on me. His stance tightens, subtly, as if his senses are on high alert. Usually, not something I would notice in anyone else, but I've been serving him for months now.

Okay, who am I kidding — I've been watching him all that time, too. He's not the only one who keeps their eye on people and I've never failed to notice what an attractive man he is.

Then, he walks toward me, hands in his pockets. He's removed his jacket, shirt unbuttoned halfway. Stopping just to my left, he angles his head a bit to the side, eyes filled with...amusement?

"What are you doing?"

Ever the smart-ass, I retort, "Sunbathing."

He's not amused. Scowling, he moves to stand in front of me, using one finger to tip my head up meet his eyes. "You disobeyed my request to wear a skirt, and by doing so, derailed the enjoyable evening I planned for us. Why is that?"

Here I am, sitting completely nude in front of a man, and he wants to discuss my choice of clothing?

Fine.

I bring my arms up, crossing them over my breasts as I glare at him. "Tell me what is the point of trapping a woman into marriage by holding her business over her head if you only intend for said marriage to end in a year?"

And, cue the return of his merriment.

He chuckles and moves to sit next to me. "Is that what

this is about? Now you tell me why that bothers you, considering you don't want to marry me in the first place."

I open my mouth, then close it again.

Damn him.

"We'll discuss this later." He grins and pats his lap. "Right now, I need to smack your ass."

I want him to smack it. Chances are, the smacking will turn into fucking, and after three days with no sex, I'm more or less ready to beg for it. But I can't let him know that.

So much for being obedient.

"I don't think so."

Grinning wider, he pulls me onto his lap. There is no struggle, as we both know I'm no match against his strength.

He adjusts my body across his legs, making it necessary for me to use my arms to brace against the floor to keep balanced. Chuckling, he caresses my ass with one hand while the other holds tightly onto my legs, making it impossible for me to wiggle.

Hit me!

I want his hands on me in a bad, I-haven't-been-fucked in days kinda way. Even if it's in spanking form.

Please, please touch me more! If I weren't trying to act like I didn't want this, that's what I would say right now.

"Safe word?"

He's worse than a woman sometimes. I don't even talk this much!

Releasing an irritated sigh, I think for a moment and then laugh. "Oompa Loompa."

The caressing stops.

He makes a sound somewhere between a cough and a chuckle. "What?"

I deliberately misinterpret his question. "Yeah. You know, from Willy Wonka?"

He smacks my ass, and I yelp before grinning. What's better is that he can't see my face, which makes this even more fun than I could've imagined.

"Let's try this again." He goes back to fondling me. "Are you sure that's the word you want to use?"

"Absolutely. It's perfect. An unsexy safe word. Especially since nobody thinks an Oompa Loompa is sexy."

His hand grips one cheek as he busts out laughing.

"Oompa Loompa it is." His hand leaves my ass. "Ten smacks."

I barely have time to process it, let alone ask why ten when he lands a firm slap on the right side.

The thing about having my ass hit is that even when I expect it to happen, I'm still shocked when contact is made. My instinct is to gasp, to try and wiggle away, despite how much I want more. But his grip is unyielding, as is the hand that lands again on the left side this time.

It doesn't hurt. If anything, I find it thrilling. I've been turned on since I first laid eyes on him this evening.

A third smack. A fourth.

I shut my eyes, the pleasure and slight sting from his hand rushing through my body. Up, up, up until it hits my brain.

Five.

I really hope he's counting.

Six.

My body is wound tight, practically humming with desire.

Seven.

Eight.

His voice interrupts, low and guttural. "Spread your legs."

I rush to oblige, conscious of what he's about to do.

"Wider."

I moan, doing as bid with enthusiasm. He runs his hand down between my legs, teasing then removes it, leaving me bereft and wanting to weep with need.

One second passes.

Two.

Three.

I yelp when his slap makes contact with my pussy. Restraining myself with every bit of energy I possess, my legs quiver as they tire of this position already.

He strokes my back, gliding his hand up until he wraps

my hair around his fist and pulls my head up. My hands leave the ground, my legs shaking harder at the extra effort needed.

"You should see your ass. It's red as can be." His other hand rubs me, a sob escaping my throat. "Delicious."

I don't know how many seconds pass as I wait, keeping my body as relaxed as possible. I'm so turned on I know one touch will send me over the edge.

I also trust he will give it to me.

My senses are so attuned at this moment that I hear his hand swinging through the air just seconds before it makes contact with my pussy once final time.

And I scream while orgasming, my whole body shaking with so much force I grip his leg with my hands to hold on.

When I go limp, he lifts me up and places me in the center of the bed. I watch as he divests himself of his clothes, then welcome him with open arms as he joins me. He kisses me, melding his mouth to mine as his cock enters me in one swift thrust.

I wrap my legs around him to bring him closer. Keeping his cock inside me, he goes immobile, leaving my mouth to trail kisses down my jaw and onto my neck. Then, using one arm to brace himself, he uses the other to cup a breast, taking the nipple in his mouth and sucking hard.

When he pauses to thrust, I moan, sliding my hands up

to grip his hair. He returns to giving my body his undivided attention, moving to the other breast to do the same. Having his cock inside me unmoving is torture, though. Just as I'm about to beg for him to move, his lips come back to mine, and he thrusts.

I whimper as his hand moves up to my neck, resting lightly against my throat as he dominates my mouth with his.

Each plunge of his cock is met with a lift of my hips, my legs tightening around him, begging for more. I disentangle one hand from his hair to slide it in between our bodies, to find where we're connected, before touching my own body in just the right way.

The noise he makes into my mouth is indistinguishable, his hand tightening around my neck just enough to send me over the edge.

It's not long before he follows me with a whisper of my name into what I consider the best bliss in the world.

A girl could get used to this.

CHAPTER TEN

"I HAVE TO RETURN HOME. MY PAPA WILL BE WAITING *for me."*

I don't want to leave him. He's my friend — my only friend. Papa doesn't let me visit with children from other families. He says they are all heathens and not fit for proper company.

So when I met the stable masters' son, who is only a few years older than me, we became instant friends in our mutual loneliness.

It wasn't long before that friendship turned to love.

Love I know my father would never approve of. I am several years away from being old enough to marry, but I am positive I will never love anyone as I do Thomas.

"Jane," he whispers, tucking a disobedient strand of black hair behind my ear, "I hate how we must sneak around. I wish our love mustn't remain a secret. I desire you

and ardently dream of you being my wife, where you may sleep in my bed."

His words make me blush.

"Kiss me then."

My words are daring, yet I know he loves when I am bold.

His dark eyes don't widen in shock. Instead, they blacken with desire, with a passion I know burns for me and me alone. I know he wants to tackle me to the grass, lift my skirts, and plunge deep inside me until we are so connected we shall never be torn apart.

No distance between us ever again, even when we are out of reach of one another.

He does as I demand.

Passion ignites. Even though I know I must leave, I take one more moment with him.

One more second where our lips combine in a fervor, we cannot and do not want to deny. One that leaves us aching for each other.

And when he pulls back, I see the regret he must leave in his eyes.

I know he loves me.

My papa is wrong.

And as Thomas walks away from me, I vow in my heart to do whatever it takes for us to be together the rest of our lives.

Only he vanishes, never to be seen again.

THE SOUND OF AN ALARM JOLTS ME OUT OF MY SLEEP, the dream disappearing before I can make sense of it.

Opening my eyes to a pitch dark room, I wonder where I am for a second before I remember.

I slept at Tobias' place.

Even more, I slept with him. Again.

Now, he'll always be my first 'second time', and I'm not sure how to feel about that.

His phone lights up from his side of the bed, the shrill tones making me wince as I finally notice that his arm is across my chest, pinning me down. And the same for his leg.

Matter of fact, if he got any closer, he'd be lying on top of me.

Mortified, I realize we fell asleep right after sex when he snuggled up against me, and exhaustion meant I hadn't stayed awake long enough to push him away.

Ugh! Snuggling!

Not sure whether to laugh or cry at this discovery, I poke his arm as the phone peals again. "Hey, wake up. Your phone is pissing me off."

He doesn't move.

The phone goes off once more.

He snores.

What's a girl to do?

I scream as loud as possible, and he jerks upright.

"What—?" His hand grabs my arm. "Joce—?"

God, I love the way he says my name. I especially enjoyed the way he moaned it last night as he came, the low growl in my ear filled with his desire and a contentment I didn't understand.

"I'm fine." I yank my arm away as the phone trills. "Shut that thing off, will you?"

Climbing out of the bed, I head to the door, using my arms to guide my way and prevent any stumbles in this unfamiliar territory. I glance over at Tobias, his face illuminated by the screen as he taps on it with his thumb. With his other hand, he swipes down his face, no doubt trying to recover from his rude awakening.

Reaching the door, I glare at him. "What fucking time is it, anyway?"

He laughs, returning the phone to its previous position on the nightstand. "Four. Forgot to change my alarm."

Oh, I want to kill him right now.

Turning the knob, I leave to use the bathroom, and return a few minutes later. Picking up my cell, I click on the flashlight to search the floor for my clothes.

"What are you doing?" His mumbled words come out of nowhere. "Get back in bed."

"Don't be demanding." Huffing, I swipe up my discarded shirt. "We're not even married yet."

"So? Get back in bed. It's early."

"Maybe it's early for you, mister 'I-can-afford-to-sleep-in.'" Squinting because the light hurts my eyes, I continue looking around for my underwear. "But since I need to go in at six anyway, I might as well stay awake."

Since my experience with men only involves one-night stands and my friend Dexter, I err on the side of Dexter and assume I'm exasperating Tobias when he sighs.

Then, he claps his hands, and the lights turn on.

I cover my eyes with my arm. "Asshole. The light is too bright!"

No point in wasting time by clapping my hands to turn them back off. He'll just do it again.

"You'll adjust. Just use one eye at first and slowly open the other," he responds with a chuckle. "Also, you need to get a manager to either open or close the diner. No need to work yourself to death."

"You know I can't afford it." Grumbling, I lower my arm and begin dressing for the day. "I don't understand why you'd even suggest such a thing."

"I didn't get where I am by doing it all myself. You need help."

That's his parting shot as he gets up and exits the room. I finish putting on my clothing and look down at my phone to see a text from Iris.

'C u in the morning. Hope u get some so u are less grumpy.'

I laugh at her use of a 'u' in place of you, something she

does deliberately because she knows it bugs me. I don't text her back since she'll be up when I get home.

Tobias returns to the room in all his naked glory. He must've gotten a quick shower, his hair dripping water onto his shoulders. Watching the beads of liquid roll down his chest has me licking my lips, wanting to touch him with my tongue. No work. We will just get naked once more, climb back in the bed, and stay there fucking until the sun comes up — the one thing I love more than anything else in the world.

He must have the same idea. Before I can blink, he's across the room and gathering me in his arms. He lowers his lips to mine, invading my mouth with a force he seems unable to subdue. Because he catches me when I'm wishing I can be all over him, I don't resist throwing my arms around his neck and returning the passionate kiss, matching his tongue stroke for stroke. We're both battling for control; something neither of us really have around the other.

Especially since I've given in to the inevitable even if I haven't agreed to it out loud.

Marriage.

Sex more than once with the same man.

I can't escape what will happen, so I may as well enjoy this while it lasts.

Because everything always ends badly.

Where the hell had that thought come from?

Before I can examine the answer, he rips his mouth from mine in such an abrupt fashion I would have stumbled if it weren't for his arms around me. Arms that leave me seconds later as he steps back.

"We should get going. Give me two minutes."

He turns away at my nod.

I race from the room, ignoring the craving for his cock and the desire to give reality the finger as temptation makes me drag him back to bed.

CHAPTER ELEVEN

Ten minutes later, we're on our way to my place, and Tobias starts in on the manager thing at the first stop light.

"Let me hire another person to help you."

I turn my head his way and glare even though he can't see me because it is almost pitch black inside the car and out.

Then, I pause because if he wants to insist, the best course of action for this topic is to take advantage.

"Okay, sure."

His laugh is short and full of disbelief. "Right. Something tells me there is a but...?"

"Smart man."

He really is which is unnerving because he knows me so well already.

"Well?"

I take a deep breath before letting it out slowly. "If you think I need help, fine. But I get to choose who to hire, and you will pay them."

"No problem. I will send you some qualified candidates today so you can interview them."

I want to object, perfectly able to find people myself, but it will be faster to let him assist me. "People who have applied to work with you, I'm guessing?"

"Smart woman."

God, he's such a wise-ass.

I love it.

"There is something else I'd like to discuss with you." His hand finds mine and curls around my fingers so I can't pull away. "Rules."

Excuse me?

"What?" is what I say out loud.

He chuckles. "Rules. I assume since you played along last night you are comfortable with a submissive role. Am I wrong?"

Oh, I see. Time to have fun with this.

"What is this exactly? *Fifty Shades of Grey*, take two?"

"No. Unlike Christian, my sanity is intact. And I'm much more attractive. Wouldn't you agree?"

Yes, he is, but I will hardly feed into his ego. Instead, I bring one finger up to my mouth and purse my lips.

"Hold on, I need to consult my inner Goddess." I

pause a beat, then retort, "She says I could probably do better."

"Tell your inner Goddess she's a dumb ass." He pulls his hand away with a laugh and rests it on my shoulder. "Now, am I wrong?"

I sigh. "No, you're not."

"Good." He squeezes my hand. "First, never wear undergarments when around me."

"Never?"

"Never, unless you'd like them ripped off your body."

Just like that, I wish his cock was inside me right this second and clench my thighs together. "What's number two?"

"You will tell me where you are going at all times."

Oh, hell no!

"I will not—"

"Jocelyn." He cuts me off, raising his voice to make sure I hear him. "This isn't about controlling you. It's about making sure I know where you are and with whom, so if anything happens or I need you, there isn't any time waste because I'm trying to figure out where you've gone."

"But I go nowhere!"

"Then it shouldn't be a problem, correct?"

I look out the window, not answering. I want to tell him I'm not sure, but don't need to. He knows me; he's aware asking such a thing will make me anxious. I'm not used to restrictions or needing to consider someone else's feelings.

"Yes or no, Jocelyn."

"I—" Squeezing my eyes shut, I grit my teeth, not knowing how to tell him how afraid I am to give in even a bit.

"Don't be afraid." He speaks softly, his tone soothing. "We both know the submissive is the one who truly holds all the power, Joce."

Yet again, he's right. I have the power to stop this, even if I lose my diner. He's not making me; he's offered me a choice.

But how does he do it? How does he speak straight to my fear when I haven't given voice to it? Am I so transparent?

"Okay." He presses my shoulder before removing his hand. "I mean, no, it's not a problem."

Noticing we're getting close to my place, with street lamps illuminating the way, I look over at him with a raised brow. "Anything else?"

"Yes." He tosses a glance my way. "However, we can discuss it later."

Pulling up to the curb in front of my place, he parks the car and leans over the middle. Our noses are near to touching as he speaks.

"I'll send over a few applicants today. All are qualified with clean backgrounds. Hire one and show them the ropes today." I nod, and he grins, his face lighting up as he gives my lips a peck. "Then, I'll see you at eight. Pack a bag for the weekend."

I jerk back a little. "What for?"

"We're going out of town." He slides his hand around my neck and brings my face close to his once more. "I've a bit of a surprise."

"But the diner—"

"It will be fine. I'm sure you can have Molly keep watch. Trust people to do it right even when you're not around."

I hate that he's right, that he's trying to help me, yet all I want to do is fight him every step of the way. He's the more successful business person between the both of us at this point; I should trust his judgment. I know I'm simply afraid to let go of any control.

I scowl at him, unwilling to admit that to him in any way, shape, or form.

"Are we getting married, Joce? I know I said you had a week to answer, but I'd like to know."

Although I've agreed in my head, it's different to say 'yes' in verbal form. It's so real. Final.

So I give him an answer in true Luna style.

"What do you think? I don't sleep with just anyone more than once."

His response is to grin and cover my mouth with his, skimming his tongue along my lips until I acquiesce.

I moan with pleasure as he conquers my mouth like he did my body the night before. Truly, he's the best kisser I've ever encountered. He's slow and steady. Each stroke of his tongue is a deliberate loving of my mouth that makes my body tremble with desire. I could kiss him for hours, doing nothing else, and be perfectly content.

And at that thought, I pull away, giving myself a mental bitch slap.

His eyes glint with humor as he lets me go. "Yummy. See you at eight."

"Got it."

That's all I say before hightailing it out of his car; not wondering where we're going this weekend, but how I'll survive being around him that long without bursting into flames.

Something tells me I'm gonna find out rather quick.

❦

"Are you sure you'll be all right?"

Molly frowns at me. "Yes, I'm sure we'll be fine. You said she comes highly recommended, right?"

"Yes." I turn to look out into the dining room, where my new manager is talking to a customer. "She's definitely qualified."

"Then stop worrying. I'll keep an eye on her. Go enjoy a weekend with that sexy fiancé of yours!"

Molly's excitement is palpable. At first, she didn't believe me this morning when I told her everything, yet somehow, in the eight hours since, she's supported me one-hundred percent.

I don't know whether I should worry that everyone in my life seems perfectly okay with me throwing myself at the big bad wolf like a succulent piece of meat.

"Yeah, I'll try." I grimace at the meat thought. "I don't even know where we're going."

Molly laughs. "Sounds like you got one that likes to keep you in a constant state of anticipation."

Oh, if she only knew.

My phone beeps, letting me know about a new text message.

Molly's eyes light up. "Speak of the devil, I bet it's him!"

Yep, she's right.

His message is to the point. '*Am I picking you up from work or your place?*'

'*Work. I brought my bag with me just in case.*'

The new manager — her name is Nicole — joins us in the back.

She grins at me, her green eyes shining. "Thanks again for hiring me! I won't let you down."

Even though I know she's older than me by five years, her enthusiasm makes her seem younger.

"See you don't," I respond with an equally nice smile.

"Your continued employment here is based on how things are going when I come back in on Monday morning."

She nods. "Yes, of course, Ms. Bates."

Another message pops up from Tobias. *'I'm outside. Let's go!'*

"Well, how rude," I mutter. "Guess he's in a hurry."

"Go, go!" Molly practically shoos me out of the room, picking up my bag and handing it over.

"Have a nice weekend!"

The parting shot is from Nicole as I head out the door, taking a deep breath while hoping the diner is still standing on my return.

CHAPTER TWELVE

AFTER THE FIRST COUPLE MINUTES OF MUNDANE chit-chat, I ask the question that's been bugging me all day.

"Where are we going?"

We are heading out of town, I know that much. The further we go, the more nervous I become.

"Promise you won't jump out of the car first."

I laugh at the unexpected comment. "Sure, I promise. Jumping out of vehicles isn't really my style no matter the situation."

"Good." He reaches over and takes my hand in his, his tone casual and nonchalant. "We're going to my parents' house."

I freeze. My heart thumps, mouth going dry.

"Breathe, Jocelyn."

Easy for him to say. He isn't the one who feels like

something suddenly hit them in the chest with a two-by-four.

"I'm not ready!"

He chuckles, lifting my hand to his mouth and kissing the back. "Nobody ever is. But you've got a wedding to plan, and they're the perfect people to help."

"What?" The kiss distracts me, just as I'm sure he hoped it would. "We don't need anything big—"

"Yes, we do. Sort of. My mother wouldn't have it any other way. You'll see what I mean."

I'm speechless.

Totally fucking never-happened-before speechless.

My head is spinning.

Relationship.

Marriage.

Sex with the same person more than once.

Meeting his parents.

Meeting his family.

Oh god, how can he expect me not to panic?

I'm breaking every rule I've ever implemented into my life.

Too fast! Everything is changing way too fast!

But there is nothing I can do; I need him.

No, I need his money.

He just comes along with it. Without him, there is no saving my diner.

Fuck!

"Do they know about...?"

"About our deal? No. I don't think there is any reason they should know that. Do you?"

"So you are okay with them thinking we're so in love we decided to marry before they even met me?" When he nods, I exclaim, "We haven't even set a date!"

"Three weeks."

My mouth drops open. He can't be serious. "You want to get married in three weeks? Are you insane?"

"I know it appears that way, but let me assure you, I'm not."

Honestly questioning his sanity, I yank my hand out of his and cross my arms over my chest. "No way! Three weeks is way too soon."

"Is it? I'm certain you have six weeks from that date on the letter to either pay the bank the money, or they will take the diner. Correct?"

Tears spring to my eyes. "Yes. I received that nearly two weeks ago."

"Precisely. And under the agreement, we must be married in order for me to pay off the debts for you."

There is always a moment when you give in to the inevitable, whatever it may be. Whether it's a choice you've brought upon yourself, a choice thrust upon you by another, or one made when you must decide between what needs done and what you will do.

I've just reached that moment.

What was it I had thought about him the first night we had dinner? That "if I was the type of girl to have relationships, he would be at the top of my list. Smart, funny, sexy, educated, and doing well for himself. A girl could do much worse."

Why am I fighting this so hard?

Isn't it stupid to argue when I will walk away in a year, debt-free, keeping the one thing in the world that is truly my own?

Why am I fighting him, when all he wants to do is help me, whatever his reasons?

I could question him again about why he wants to marry me, but in the end, do I even care?

No, I don't. Not really.

All I'm concerned with is saving my business. If this is what I have to do to achieve that, then so be it.

"All right," I finally respond. "Three weeks it is."

"Excellent." He tosses me a smile, then turns a corner leading to a darker road. "Anything you want to know before we get there?"

In for a penny...

"Any siblings? Will they be there? Am I going to have to milk any cows?"

"No, but I will." He chuckles. "I have a brother and sister, both younger. And yes, they are there already."

"Ah, oldest child. Makes sense." Then I blink at what he said. "Wait. You're going to milk a cow?"

"I might." He makes another turn, the tires crunching on gravel. "We're here."

As we drive up to the house, it's too dark out for me to see anything other than the long driveway. As he pulls into a spot on the side and parks, the front of the house becomes illuminated by lights, allowing me to view the home in all its glory.

And what a magnificent residence it is.

I stand there gaping at the size while Tobias retrieves our bags from the trunk.

His parents' home appears to be an old manor house. Made of brick with a big front door, wide bottom windows with smaller windows above on the second floor, in a T-shape design with a part that has a pointed roof.

"Charming, isn't it? Come on. Let's go inside."

Once we enter, he puts our bags down and yells to get attention. "Mom! We're here!"

At his bellow, a door opens down the hall, followed by another, and one more. First is a woman I assume is his mother. She has chin-length brown hair threaded with silver and dark brown eyes, leading the way while beaming. Behind her, a woman and man, both with similar features, and two little children who come careening around their grandmother's legs straight toward Tobias.

"Uncle 'Biath! You came!" One squeals as they both launch themselves at him. "Did you bwing pwesents?"

He picks them up easily, holding one in each arm as he turns toward me.

Then the weirdest thing happens.

His eyes meet mine, and his mouth moves, yet I don't hear what he says.

My ears buzz, brain fogging. I open my mouth, try to lift my hand, only to feel as if something is holding it down.

As my legs give out, words whisper through my mind just before I hit the floor.

"It doesn't matter if your father doesn't like me. My family will love you. Let's run away, right this instant."

WHEN I COME TO, I'M LYING ON SOMETHING SOFT, AND my head is killing me.

Before my eyes are barely open, Tobias is hovering over me, worry clouding his eyes.

"Thank fuck you're awake." He brushes my lips with his mouth. "Does your head hurt? You hit the floor before I could even react."

"Yes." I close my eyes briefly before opening them again, unable to speak above a whisper thanks to my pounding head. "Motrin?"

He nods at the side table. "Right there. Let's sit you up first."

A few minutes later, I'm sitting up, meds taken. He sits next to the bed in a chair and stares at me expectedly.

"H-how long was I out?"

"About ten minutes." He reaches for my hand, interlacing our fingers, never breaking eye contact with me. "What happened?"

Ten minutes. Wow!

I frown, unsure whether I should tell him about what I heard or not.

He must take my silence as something else, saying, "It's okay if you can't remember. All I know is I turned toward you to introduce my twin nieces, and you gave me this funny look — kind of like they confused you about something — then your eyes rolled back and down you went."

"I felt weird. Like my brain was fuzzy. That's all."

Relief sweeps through his face. "You're probably hungry. I'll order pizza."

He pulls out his phone and taps on the screen.

"Guess I made quite the impression, huh?"

"Yep." He grins as he puts the phone up to his ear. "Scared the shit out of all of 'em. You'll get fawned over in the morning."

"Can't wait."

As he talks to the pizza place, I lift a hand to the back of my head. The tender spot where my head aches only sports a small bump and my headache is already dissipating.

Maybe he's right, and I just need to eat. It has been nearly ten hours since I had any food.

I decide not to mention that or about what I heard.

After all, I'm not even sure it was while conscious, even if it felt that way.

Right as he hangs up the phone, there is a knock at the door.

"Come in."

His sister slips into the room with a gentle smile, shutting the door behind her with a soft click. Like Tobias, she has the same hair and eyes, but her face is fuller, and she's about my height. She comes to stand by the bed, next to where Tobias sits.

"Mother sent me to check up on you." She winks at me, then rests a hand on her brother's shoulder. "And you. The look on your face was epic, Toby."

Although he rolls his eyes, I can see his affection for his sister in them. "Can it, Breena. Say hello to your future sister-in-law."

Her name has me gasping, my eyes slamming shut.

"Brynja!"

We're running through the woods, hands clasped together, yelling at the top of our lungs.

"Brynja! Where are you? We must return home at once!"

He is growing frantic every second she does not answer us. And because he is, I am as well.

His sister has been gone for hours. If we do not find her soon, the worst will be assumed.

That cannot happen.

He needs her. I need her.

"Brynja, this isn't funny any longer! Show yourself!"

Someone taps my cheek.

"Jocelyn!"

I force my eyes open to find Tobias in my face. "What? I'm s-sorry. I don't know…"

Fuck, I don't even know what to say. What the hell just happened?

Breena is standing back, the corner on her face mirroring his, her lips pursed in thought.

He cups my face in his hand, forcing me to meet his gaze. "Are you all right? You looked like you passed out."

"Perhaps we should take her to the hospital," Breena suggests. "She might've hit her head harder than we think."

"No, I didn't." I put my hands in the air, palms up to indicate 'I don't know,' as I shrug. "My head doesn't hurt. I think I am starving."

I despise lying.

But I'm not sure what the hell is going on, and until I figure it out, I'm not saying one damn word.

Before they can say anything else, the doorbell rings.

Tobias releases my chin with one final look of concern,

then turns toward the door. "That'll be the pizza. I'll be right back."

Breena doesn't even give me a chance to blink before she says, "Me too! I need something to drink."

She leaves the room on his heels.

I don't care.

I'm glad to have a second to myself.

Since I'm pretty sure I'm going insane, I may not have many of those moments left.

The thought makes me chuckle.

CHAPTER THIRTEEN

After some pizza, I'm feeling much better.

Tobias throws in some random comedy movie, and we sit next to each other on the bed, watching and laughing as we eat.

At ten-thirty, as the credits roll, he announces it time for bed.

Five in the morning comes early for everyone in this house. Or so I've been warned.

I slip out of my clothes, leaving on my undies and tank, climbing into bed and under the blankets. Tobias crawls in moments later, all warm body and minty fresh breath as he snuggles against me from behind.

"How's your head?" He follows up the question with a kiss by my ear, then down on my neck. "All better?"

"Mm, it's fine."

He slides one arm under my neck, the other coming

around to haul my body closer to his. The pecks grow more firm, into the crook of my neck, followed by my shoulder. He grinds against me, his cock stiff and ready to go. I sigh softly as he continues to tease me.

"I know it's been a long day, but…"

Men! They're all the same.

I would say no if I really didn't want it. But, his touch, his kisses, and the promise of having his cock inside me in just a few moments is too much to resist.

However, if he wants sex, he will have put effort into it.

Do all the work that is.

"Yes, it has," I respond softly. "I'm not moving. I'm comfy."

The hand keeping my lower body pressed against his slips beneath the band of my panties and down to my pussy as he snickers against my shoulder. "No problem, Joce. You simply lay there and enjoy. I love pleasing you."

"If you keep talking, I'll fall asleep, and you won't get to do anything, let alone please me."

He slides the underwear down my legs where I kick them off.

His hand comes back to teasing me, two fingers sliding up and down between my lips, making me squirm. The arm around my neck moves down to under my torso, where he uses it to bring our bodies flush, as close as two people can be. He sneaks his hand under my tank and fondles my

THE SEDUCTION OF LUNA

breast, rolling the nipple between his fingers, causing it to pebble before pinching it.

I moan, his action simultaneous with the penetration of his two fingers.

"You're so wet for me already." He pulls out slightly, then thrusts them back in, his thumb toying with my clit. "Fuck. I need to be inside you."

That's what I need, too.

"Do you want my cock buried in you, Joce?" At my nod, he nips my ear. "Say it. Tell me how much you want it."

Removing his fingers, I sob at the loss. "Please. I need your cock inside of me. Fuck me, please. I want you to fuck me now."

He positions himself perfectly, pushing into me inch by inch, without me having to move position at all.

He continues to play with me as he fucks me, each plunge of his cock on the border between gentle and firm, yet swift. I cover my mouth with my arm to stifle my moans and whimpers of pleasure. With my legs together, I feel every inch of him and the pleasure makes me clench around him.

"Do it again," he demands, moaning in bliss as I oblige. "Damn, that's hot. I love when you squeeze around me like that, as if your pussy is hugging my cock."

I'm incoherent as I climax, clenching around him involuntarily. His grip around my body tightens as he speeds up, my body going limp until finally, he comes with a muffled moan of his own.

I lift a hand and tap his in a reassuring manner. "I'm glad you like my cock hugs."

The last thing I recall before falling asleep is him chuckling.

THEY ARE DRAGGING HIM AWAY FROM ME.

His eyes never leave mine. He struggles, but we both know all hope is lost.

We will never be together.

I sob as I'm held back by my brothers, unable to run after him. Unable to give him one final kiss.

Then suddenly, they stop walking, and my entire insides fill with dread.

One of the three men holding him pulls out a knife and stands behind him.

I open my mouth as I scream, yet no sounds emerge.

His stare holds mine, shining with love and defiance, completely aware that his life is about to meet the end.

I know why they do this. They have big plans. Plans for me to marry a wealthy and very influential man. They do not want me with him because he can do nothing for them except love me.

Why won't they let me be loved?

In my peripheral vision, I see my aunt step forward. I don't look her way. My gaze never leaves my beloved.

Her voice rings out, every line of the curse she reads bone-chilling:

> *Seven lives you shall spend,*
> *Searching every corner and bend;*
> *The one you seek never far,*
> *Yet still distant as a star.*

> *Lessons you shall learn*
> *Without them, you will burn;*
> *Never to escape the heat*
> *Unless together your two hearts beat.*

> *Every obstacle in your way,*
> *Means neither of you stay;*
> *Without the other to cherish,*
> *Forever you shall perish.*

They place the knife at his throat, and that is when the scream rips from my throat, piercing the air with my anger and grief.

I'm forced backward with a hand over my mouth as Þórsteinn's piercing gaze softens, his mouth lifting up in one last smile just for me as he shouts, "Ek elska þik, Jórunnr!"

"I love you, too!"

But he doesn't hear me, my face shoved into my brother's chest and held there as they murder him without my witness. And when I am released, my grief gives way to insanity, taking over my actions. I grab my brother's knife and place the tip against my neck, moving away quick while keeping them all in my line of vision and shriek, "How dare you? If I cannot have him, then you cannot have me!"

And before they can react to stop me, I smile at the thought of joining my love in death, then stab myself in the place where I will bleed out.

It's not long before the world goes black.

❦

I WAKE UP GASPING FOR BREATH.

Lifting my hands up to my neck, I pat around the sides and down my chest, reassuring my brain it was all a dream.

A sick, twisted trick of my mind, replacing the face of a man who gets his head cut off with Tobias. And has me killing myself over his death.

Only in my dreams will I ever be so devoted to one man.

I toss aside the covers while noticing two things: the sun is shining brightly... and Tobias isn't in bed.

I figured he would wake me up, but then again, I did scare the shit out of him last night. Twice.

Grimacing, I get out some clothing and head to the bathroom to take a shower, wishing I could make sense of what has happened enough to bring it up to Tobias without sounding as if I am crazy.

As the hot water runs through my hair and down my body, I think about the dream I had last night once more.

I remember his name — Þórsteinn — and what had he called the girl? Jórunnr, that's it. What had he yelled at her? Ek elska þik. "I love you, too," she had replied.

What language is that? I must look it up later.

Well, if I can figure out how to spell it.

Then, there's the poem.

Just thinking about it gives me chills, causing me to shiver as if I'm not standing under water hot enough to burn.

I've never been much of a dreamer nor one to have nightmares. At least, not since I was a child.

And to "dream" of things while awake like I had last night freaks me out more than I can possibly articulate. I hadn't been sleeping as they thought; it had felt like a memory slamming its way back into my mind, like a long-lost friend calling you out of the blue one day.

I know that seems insane.

I'm not remembering these things as if they

happened to me. They are long ago, in different worlds, with different names.

Apparently, Tobias is making me crazy in more ways than one.

Once I finish in the shower, I step out and get dressed.

When I'm standing in front of the mirror, brushing my hair, I notice a mark I've always that catches my attention and touch it with one finger.

The mark isn't huge. As I examine it in the mirror, a real memory from my childhood surfaces.

"Daddy, what's this?"

He picks me up and places me on his knee, examining the spot I point to on my neck, then chuckles softly. "It's just a birthmark sweetie. It's hardly noticeable."

"But what is it? Why is it there?"

"Well, I don't want to scare you, Luna. Just know you're beautiful no matter what."

"You won't scare me, Daddy. Tell me, please!"

He looks at me for a long moment, my excitement to learn something new reflected in his eyes as he ponders whether or not to tell me. I know he's trying to make sure I don't change my mind, but I'm a stubborn girl. I don't like to give in — and neither does he.

However, I win when he resigns with a smile. "You asked why it's there. Well, one theory I've heard is that it's a mark showing how you died in a previous life."

I gasp with all the indignation a nine-year-old can

muster as I'm not sure what to say, and he chuckles, ruffling my hair.

"Go play sweetie. It's just a mark. Nothing to worry yourself over."

Shaking my head, I roll my eyes and put the brush down.

Much as I loved my father, I don't believe in past lives nor do I believe a birthmark is a remnant of how you died before.

However, I do believe in eating breakfast, and damn, I'm starving.

So I head downstairs hoping not to get lost on the way because I've no idea where the kitchen is.

CHAPTER FOURTEEN

Fuck, I'm lost.

A reasonable person would think heading down a hallway toward steps would lead them to the floor below. Then taking those steps down after determining the current location is on the second floor, the person would end up on the first floor.

All things I assume.

Not true.

Somehow I end up going through a door that leads to the outside into what looks like a garden.

When I go to head back inside, I find the entryway locked.

And I left my phone upstairs.

Great.

I can see this will be an awesome day.

That is about fifty percent sarcasm.

After all, it appears to be a lovely area.

There is a huge water fountain in the middle straight ahead, with three white benches around it. Lots of trees; what kind, I have no clue. It looks as if they fenced the area in, so I head to the left, hoping to find another way inside.

Rounding the corner, I am nearly run into by the twins, who squeal and attach themselves to my legs.

I laugh. "Well, hey there you two. Are you out here all alone?"

They look up at me grinning, eyes shining with mischief. I gather they are about four years old; not that I know much about children.

"We run from mommy! We play hide-n-seek!"

Okay, they're cute, I'll give them that.

Releasing my legs as I crouch down, I smile into each of their dark brown eyes. "I'm lost. Will you help me get back inside?"

Both nod enthusiastically and take a hand on either side of me. A moment or two later, we round a corner and their mother stops us.

"There you are!" Breena smiles at me. "Thanks for returning them. I'm not worried about them getting out since there is only one gate." She points to the one behind her. "However, I still hate when they run off."

"Actually, they were helping me. I thought I was heading toward the kitchen and somehow ended up out here. I didn't know how to get out."

She bursts out laughing. "That'll happen a lot in this house. Make sure you have your phone with you from here on out so my brother can rescue you." She holds her hands out to the girls. "Come on, you two. Let's show Jocelyn the kitchen and get ourselves something to eat, hmm?"

They giggle and release my hands, running to take hers.

"What are their names?"

"I'm Tabitha," one says with a toothy grin, pointing at the other, "and she's Beatrice."

I nod as Breena leads them away, and I follow.

T and B.

Tabitha and Beatrice.

Tobias and Breena.

Had she given the siblings the same initials as her and her brother on purpose?

They seem close. I don't know why it bothers me like it does.

I just can't seem to shake the feeling I'm missing something.

What that is I don't have the slightest clue.

So I push it aside to examine later as we enter the house.

His mother is at the stove as we walk in. She

turns as the girls laugh, taking seats at the little table in the corner while screaming, "Hi gwandma!"

"You two ready for breakfast?" She places their plates in front of the two kids as they bob their heads and then she turns toward me. "And how are you this morning?"

"Oh, I'm fine, thank you."

Breena takes a seat at the counter and pats the stool next to her. "Come eat. We don't need a repeat of last evening."

Man, she's bossy.

I sit down anyway, hoping Tobias will walk in at any second and save me from being alone with his mother and sister.

It's one thing to meet the family; it's another to face them alone.

"Where's Tobias?" I ask as she sets a plate in front of me.

Two eggs, two slices of bacon, and two big strawberries. My stomach growls at the sight.

Breena laughs. "He's out chopping wood with dad and our brother. They'll be in in a few minutes."

My fork pauses halfway to my mouth, which is now hanging open. "Chopping wood? As in, with an axe?" Duh, Jocelyn, of course it's with an axe! "Sorry, stupid question."

The mental image of Tobias shirtless, sweating from

the exertion of his activity, replaces my appetite for food with an intense desire to get him naked again.

I no longer have to wonder where he gets his physical form and stamina from. Apparently, the man milks cows and chops wood on the weekends. I bet he rides horses and rescues cats from trees, too.

Who would've thought? Not me, that's for certain, even after he told me about growing up in the country.

His mother's hand covers the one I have resting on the counter. "Not stupid. You look shocked, though. Didn't Tobias tell you he grew up on a farm?"

"No." I shake my head and put the fork down. "He said he grew up in the country, that's all."

She clucks her tongue, giving my hand a squeeze before turning away. "Don't pay him any mind. He likes to keep people guessing."

"Yeah, I know, trust me."

"How did you two meet?" Breena asks.

I glance at her. "He didn't tell you?"

"Sure he did. It doesn't mean it's always true, though. He loves to exaggerate."

Now that I didn't know.

Before I can answer, the door opens and in walks our topic of conversation. Right behind him are his dad and brother. They are scarcely inside when Tabitha and Beatrice shriek with excitement, "Uncle 'Biath!" and run toward him.

"Whoa, whoa, girls!" They stutter to a halt in front of him. "Uncle Tobias is dirty. Let me go clean up first, all right?"

He looks over at the counter, and seeing me, grins.

I admit, I love when he smiles at me. His whole face lights up, and he gazes at me as if I'm the only woman in the world he wants. Which is crazy since I'm sure he could have his pick?

Whatever, though. If marrying me is what he wants, that's just what he'll get. Relationship challenged Jocelyn who can't even find her way out of a bedroom in a house without getting lost.

Heading toward me, I register he is not wearing a shirt mere seconds before his lips descend on mine, kissing me in front of everyone. It's brief, yet long enough I will definitely follow him up the steps to jump his bones. He draws back.

"Morning, babe."

Oh, now he uses an endearment for the first time, and in front of his parents no less. Needless to say, I can't resist taking it to the next level — unspoken challenge accepted!

"How goes it, munchkin?"

His whole family roars with laughter as he takes my chin in his hand and kisses me again, chuckling against my mouth.

"I can tell this one's got your number, bro. You better watch out."

I turn my head to look toward the voice, finally inspecting his brother. A younger version of Tobias with enough differences to imply their relation to each other without mistaking them for twins. Same brown hair and brown eyes as everyone else, identical impish grin as Tobias.

Then, I look at his father — only to see he has blue eyes and blond hair — and my eyes widen in surprise.

He catches my eye and winks. "Amazing isn't it? Not one of them got my coloring."

They all laugh again, and I'm embarrassed, realizing many people must react the way I did.

"Aren't you going to introduce us, Toby?" His brother pipes up.

I elbow him in the side. "Yeah, Toby, introduce us."

"Okay, okay!" He groans and inclines his head as he introduces each one. "This is my father Sven, my brother Randolf with an F, and my mother, Liv."

For some reason, his specification of 'with an F' for his brother's name amuses me, and I smile. "Sven, Randolf with an F, and Liv. Got it. Nice to meet you all."

"You too, hon," his mother says before glaring at the men. "Now you guys go clean up and get back down here for some breakfast."

Tobias gives me a peck on the lips. "Be back in ten."

I stand up. "Take me with you. I need to know how to get there and back since I got lost this morning."

I also plan to fuck him in the shower after he washes off, but I won't give voice to that in front of everyone.

"Did you?" He laughs, his desire to do the same clear in the hot look he gives me. "All right, come on. You can tell me all about the trip on our way upstairs."

As we leave the room, I look back to find his whole family watching us, smiles on each and every one of their faces.

I take that as a good sign.

And hate they think there is so much more to this relationship than actually exists.

CHAPTER FIFTEEN

THE QUESTIONS ABOUT WHAT WE WOULD LIKE TO DO for our wedding arrive halfway through dinner.

Sven is at one end of the table, Liv at the other, with Breena and Randolf on one side of the table. Tobias and I sit on the other side while the twins are at their own little table.

His mother is the one to introduce the topic. "Where do you want the wedding to take place?"

"Well..." Tobias keeps his eyes on me as he responds. "I'm hoping we can have it here, now that Jocelyn has seen the place."

Smooth way to put me on the spot, but I'll do whatever he wants as long as he does what I need him to do.

Other than giving me multiple orgasms, that is.

I nod. "Sure. I would love for it to take place in the garden, personally."

Breena interjects with, "Isn't that kind of small, though? How many people will you invite?"

Tobias reaches for my hand under the table and squeezes it. "A small wedding with all of us and a few friends would be perfect."

I look down.

Figures he would know I have no family; that it's me, myself and I. And I know they are taking what he said and realizing the same thing, but I don't want or need their pity.

Lifting my head back up, I smile brightly. "And, we've got just shy of three weeks to plan it."

That has them all gasping and safely moves the topic away from my lack of relatives.

"Knocked up, huh?" His brother comments. "Shocking."

Tobias throws his roll at Randolf's head as I direct an 'told you so' look at my soon-to-be husband. "No, asshole. We simply don't want to wait."

"Riiiight. If you say so."

His mother taps the table to get everyone's attention. "In that case, there's no time to waste, is there?"

"I will give Jocelyn your number, Mom. That way you two can talk once we're back in town." His phone rings and he grimaces while gazing at the screen. "Excuse me, I need to take this. Sorry."

Breena glances at me with sympathy. "Better get used

to it. I swear that phone is glued to his ear. Hopefully getting married will give him something else to focus on."

If only she knew how much he already focuses on me. Any more and I'll probably scream.

I smile at her, not knowing what else to do, and unable to say what I want.

The topic swiftly returns to wedding plans alongside the washing up as I wonder what the call he got could possibly be about.

And why it is taking so long for him to return.

⚜

WE'RE IN A ROOM ALL ALONE, THE SOUNDS OF LAUGHTER *and music floating through the closed door.*

He turns from the fireplace and grins at me. "You look beautiful this evening. I wish we were truly alone, instead of hiding in this room. I want nothing more than to know what you look like naked underneath that dress."

"You know my papa would never allow that," I say with a smile of my own. "You must marry me if you wish such a thing."

He stalks toward me, his beautiful dark gaze never leaving my silver-blue eyes. When he reaches me, he gathers me in his arms, his lips crushing mine.

I know it's improper, yet I cannot help but to return his kiss with equal passion.

Ever since we met a few weeks ago, we have been unable to stay apart. Every dance or gathering we both attend is spent in each other's arms in some room far from the others.

We are bound to get caught, but I am unable to care.

I know he's the one for me. And he knows that I am the one for him.

Now we just needed our mothers and fathers to agree.

He keeps saying he waits for the right time, and that time has not yet come.

At the discreet knock on the door, his lips left mine as we sprung away from each other.

"Come in," he commands.

The door opens, and my sister slips inside, a mischievous look in her blue eyes as she scrutinizes our closeness. I know she won't tell, though; after all, she's the one who procures us the ability to have our stolen moments together. Newly married herself, I know she's paying me back for all the occasions I helped her get some alone time with her now husband.

"We must go," she says, voice low as she focuses on me. "You've been gone too long; Mama and Papa are getting suspicious. Say your farewells until another time."

"Theo," I murmur as he envelops me in his arms once more. "I shall miss you, so much."

"And I you, Josie." He kisses my lips softly, then releases me with a sigh. "Until next time."

He nods at my sister as he heads to the door and exits, shutting the door behind him.

"He will have to ask Mama and Papa soon." I turn to the mirror to make sure all is as it should be. "I cannot stand this. He is all I want, and I am what he desires. We shall be together even if I must run away!"

My sister shakes her head. "Be patient. You know he adores you. He will ask them soon, I'm sure of it."

As we exit the room to return to the party, I'm sure he will too.

"Joce?"

My eyes flutter open as his hand touches my face. Tobias is blocking the light as he stands above me.

I lick my lips, frowning. "I must've fallen asleep. What time is it?"

"Ten. I didn't want to wake you, but we have to leave."

At that, I'm alert once more. That's when I notice the banked frustration in his eyes.

"What's wrong?"

He takes a step back as I sit up, removing his hand from my face and running it through his hair. "I need to go out of town. One of the businesses I acquired weeks ago is having issues and dealing with the crisis in person is necessary."

"Oh, I see." Sliding out from beneath the blankets, I stand up and stretch. "How long?"

"A week." He turns around and picks up his bag with a weary sigh. "Maybe two. I'll know more when I get there."

Fuck.

A week or two without him? Okay. It's not like I'm in love or something.

But no sex?

I'm pretty sure I'll die without it.

I don't say that, though. Instead, I voice a complaint that is completely legitimate for a person who isn't me.

"A week or two? That'll keep you gone up until the wedding, meaning I have to plan it all." I cross my arms over my chest. "Nice timing."

He turns and walks toward me.

"I don't want to leave." He tugs me against him, wrapping his arms around my waist. "A week or two without fucking you may kill me."

"Really?"

I can't hide my disbelief. Yes, the sex between us is great, but I didn't know he felt the same way as me.

His family is right. He does like to keep people guessing.

"God, yes." He puts his face in the crook of my neck, nipping the skin with his teeth, then sucking lightly. "Barring this trip, I hope we have sex every day for the next year; perhaps twice a day for good measure."

I curl my fingers into his arm, clinging to him. "When are you leaving?"

"Soon." He gets the hint, though. "But what's another thirty minutes when I've got my own plane?"

"Exactly."

Arousal awakens through every inch of me at his words, my pussy clenching at the knowledge he will soon be inside of me. He grins while crouching, pulling my pants and undies down at the same time. I step out of them, tugging my shirt off as he removes his clothing in tandem.

When we're both naked, I jump him. Literally.

I wrap my arms around his neck and my legs around his waist. He puts his hands on my ass as our mouth fuse together, hungry for a taste of each other that will have to last until we see each other again. He carries me over to the wall, pushing my back against it, using one hand to guide his cock into me. His hand tightens on my hips as he thrusts up and pushes me down simultaneously.

I'm glad our mouths are tangled up in each other, the feeling of his cock deep inside me causing me to cry out.

There is no gentleness in this; no mercy. His hands control the movements, his body keeps mine trapped flush against the wall, and his mouth ravages mine.

As the pleasure rises to a peak I'm sure will shatter me any second, it happens again.

"You've bewitched me, from the moment our eyes met."

Too far gone to react at the words flashing through my mind as if they are real, Tobias thrusts in just the right way, sending me over the edge.

"Nothing will ever keep us apart. My cock is yours, and your pussy belongs to me, and we fit together perfectly."

God, yes we do.

And right now, I'm glad for the wall and his body.

Holding me up when I feel like I'm falling, and I've no idea where I will land.

All I know is I better figure things out.

Fast.

CHAPTER SIXTEEN

He drops me off at my place around eleven-thirty after giving me his mother's number, reminding me about the rules, and delivering a leisurely kiss that promises many amazing pleasures upon his return.

Entering the apartment, I'm disappointed to discover both Iris and Dexter aren't here.

Heading to my room, I put away my stuff and then take a shower.

After finishing up, I head to the kitchen for some water, only to find them both in the living room. Iris is the first to see me.

"Hey, girl! Weren't you supposed to be back tomorrow?"

"Yeah, but he has some work emergency out of town he had to go deal with." I plop down beside her on the couch. "How's it going, Dex?"

He tosses me a smile, then returns to flipping through the channels. "Same old."

"I've got a question for you. Well, for both of you."

They turn their heads to look at me and I smile. "Iris, I'd like for you to be my maid of honor. And Dex, I was wondering if you'd be willing to give me away?"

And just like that, they both pounce me while squealing with excitement.

Maybe the next few weeks won't be so bad after all.

"WHAT HAVE YOU DONE?"

I storm into my father's office.

He's behind his desk writing and looks up when I come in, frowning at me. "If you are speaking of what I believe you are speaking of, I did it for you. There is no need to ruin your future over a man of no consequence."

"You have no right to decide such a thing—"

"I am your father. I have every right," he barks, standing up to move around the desk. "And as my daughter, you will do as I say, not as you please."

I'm close to the entryway. I back up as he storms toward me, fear skittering through me at the anger written all over his face. I know I may need to make a quick escape.

"Please, Father," I beg even though I know I shouldn't

as tears stream down my face, "I love him. Do not take him from me. He brings me such happiness—"

His hand strikes my face, cutting off my words as I stumble backward, falling to the floor from the force of his strike.

"He does not love you. He wants your money, you ignorant child."

I shake my head, covering the spot where he hit me with my hand as I sob, "He does love me! He does not care about the money. He said he would have me without it!"

"He took the money I offered him and ran." His words are low and filled with a hateful glee. "You know nothing. He used you and your sister."

I gasp, staring at up him through blurry eyes.

"That's right," he hisses, bending over to get close to my face. "I know all about your stolen moments with him, and how your sister aided you. Nothing gets past me."

"What money?" I whisper, all the fight in me dissipating. "How much did you give him, Father?"

"Enough." He straightens and turns around, his back to me. "Get up off the floor."

I stumble as I try to get up without assistance, my clothing making it difficult to squat as needed to rise. When I am standing once more, he is back in his chair and staring at me.

"Do you remember me telling you what would happen the next time you disobeyed me?"

I nod, unwilling to say another word for fear he will hit me again, even as the panic returns at his words.

"Then you should prepare for your wedding to a man of my choosing. You may leave me now."

He goes back to writing, and I do as he bids.

On the way to my room, I begin making plans to run away.

With or without Theo, I will stay here no longer.

THE NEXT FEW WEEKS FLY BY.

I returned to work on Sunday to keep myself occupied, only to find the diner in perfect working order.

Nicole really knows her stuff, and as the wedding preparations pick up, I'm glad to have her help.

Tobias' mother calls me every day with more decisions to make.

Then, when he and I get the chance to text, we discuss how she's driving us both insane with her questions. He doesn't talk about the work situation, instead choosing to send me random pictures of people he's dealing with making funny faces during the meetings.

And I continue to keep the disturbing yet interesting dreams to myself.

The dreams are so vivid they seem real and I'm not

sure what to make of them. Who knew I had such a terrific imagination? I didn't.

What's insane are the details. The names all start with the same letters in them all. The man's face is Tobias, and I'm the girl.

After the most recent one, I woke up to find myself sobbing, tears streaming down my cheeks, as if the sadness were my own.

As if my father had slapped me so hard I'd fallen to the floor.

And I want all of this to stop.

I don't know what the point of the dreams are, but I don't want them anymore.

I have a bad feeling the ending of the most recent one isn't one I want to know.

And later in the night, on the eve of our wedding, my feelings prove correct.

CHAPTER SEVENTEEN

I'M IN BED WHEN I HEAR A NOISE OUTSIDE THE GLASS
doors leading to my balcony.

Recognizing the secret tap we came up with many
weeks ago, I make my way over quick and quiet to let
Theo in.

His dark eyes sweep over me as he slips inside. "I was
afraid he would hurt you. I needed to see you."

"Oh!" I toss my arms around his neck, sobbing into the
crook of his shoulder as he envelops me with his. "H-he
hit me!"

"Shh." He strokes my hair as I cry. "You must stop
crying so we may make a plan to leave."

I lift my head and stare at him, eyes round. "Y-you
didn't t-take his money?"

He removes one arm from around my body, pulling out

a handkerchief and dabbing my eyes with it. After he's finished, he holds it up for me to take.

"Of course, I did." He grins mischievously. "We shall use it to start our new life."

I wipe away the remnants of my despair, happy with his plan. I have no qualms about using my father's money to start a new life with the man who loves me. If he refuses to let me be happy with Theo, while keeping him in my life, then I will happily never lay eyes upon him again.

"Where shall we go?"

He shrugs. "Anywhere. Everywhere. We will be free."

"He'll never stop looking for me." My lower lip wobbles as I imagine never being free of my father's control. "I will be a runaway and you, a criminal. But I refuse to let him choose who I'm to marry."

"We will marry." Theo slides his hand up my back to my neck, then brings his lips near mine. "I will never let you marry another. You belong to me."

His words thrill me. Just before his lips meet mine, I whisper, "And you to me."

The kiss is chaste; innocent in a way I know I haven't been in an eternity. Our mouths move against one another, our bodies flush against one another, all the promises in the world between us.

I long to undress, pressing my soft, naked form against his strength-filled one. I know from experience how he can lift me with little effort and hold me against a wall, breathing unchanged. I wonder what it would be like when I'm bared before him; how he will touch me and what words he will whisper in my ear when we finally make love.

Theo is an honorable man, for all that my father believes him not. He refuses to take me until we are husband and wife. And although I don't care either way, I still adore him all the more for it.

I pull my mouth away from his. "Let's go now. I cannot bear to stay here any longer."

He doesn't even have a chance to reply as the door to my room flies open.

Theo shoves me behind him as my father enters. My eyes widen at the sight of the revolver in his hand.

"Thought I would not guess you would try to run away with my daughter, didn't you?" He lifts his arm, pointing the gun straight at Theo. "And now, you shall die for being foolish. You should have taken the money and left my daughter alone."

"Please, Father!" I move out from behind Theo, trying to take the attention off of him as I take a step toward him. "Don't shoot him, this was my idea—"

"QUIET!" His eyes, wild with anger, find me as he keeps the gun pointed at my love. "You stupid, witless girl. You are under age. You belong to me, and you will do as I say!"

I lift my chin, defiant until the very end. "I will not. And if you kill Theo, you shall never see me again."

He laughs. "Stupid! What will you do, hmm? Take up work as a maid? You have never done even so much as dress yourself." His eyes move back to Theo, dismissing me.

Putting his hands up in the air as a sign of surrender, Theo gives me one long, heartbreaking glance before looking back at my father. "I will go peacefully. It is not my desire to make life difficult for Josie. I love her."

"You think me unintelligent? I know that unless you die, you will never leave her alone. And since you are trespassing in my unwed daughter's room, no one will find fault with me protecting her honor."

I'm frozen with fear. My father is right. Nobody will question him for shooting Theo.

I don't want to live without him.

I see my father say something, but it is lost amongst the thoughts swirling in my brain. At what my life will be if the man I love is not in it.

And when he steadies his hand and shoots to kill, I do the only thing a girl who will suffer either way would do.

As if I'm outside my body, I watch as I scream and jump in front of Theo. He shouts 'No!' but it is too late.

The bullet lodges itself in my chest as my father's eyes go wide with horror, his face draining of all color as Theo wraps me in his arms.

With my last breath, I stare up at Theo as he holds me, eyes filled with tears and gasp one final word.

"Run."

My eyes close as the darkness approaches with one final thought.

If I somehow end up living, I shall never love again.

THE MORNING OF OUR WEDDING DAWNS BRIGHTLY.

And wow, I'm not sure it's possible for me to feel worse than I do now.

I slept alone last night even though Tobias has returned. His mother insisted we must sleep apart the evening before because he shouldn't see me on our wedding day until I walk down the aisle.

I'm not happy about that and definitely not thrilled with the ending to that dream.

Nor am I elated at the fact I didn't get to have sex last night after going three weeks without.

I am ready to burst from the sexual tension running throughout me; tension not even masturbation has eased.

I want his cock inside me more than anything else.

And if it weren't for the people who will hover around me all day trying to get things ready, I would sneak off to his room for a quickie.

Soon, I chant over and over in my head. Soon you'll be all alone with him.

Sighing, I toss aside the covers and make for the shower.

Today will be a really long day.

THE MOMENT I REALIZE MY FEELINGS GO DEEPER than I originally thought arrives after my shower, while standing in front of the mirror.

I'm putting on my hose when a spot I've never seen before catches my eyes.

A barely noticeable blemish on my chest.

And yet, there it is.

In the same location as where the bullet hit the girl in my dream.

I must be seeing things because surely this isn't real.

This isn't logical and makes no sense, in any way.

Yet, I can't ignore this feeling much longer.

The dreams featuring Tobias and I in differing roles. Different names, same faces.

A poem that I'm pretty sure is a curse upon the two lovers.

Hearing phrases in his voice while we're having sex, yet he's not speaking.

His sister, whose name is eerily similar to one from the past, lost in the woods during what appears to be a memory.

The nightmares where we one of us — or both of us — die.

I'm dressing robotically as I continue to stare at my face in the mirror, pondering.

If the girl in the most recent dream is me, is that why I avoid relationships? Is that the reason I don't feel as if I can love anyone, ever?

And if it was me, if it had actually happened — and Tobias was Thomas, and Theo, and Þórsteinn — does that mean there is no one else for me?

These notions torture me as I finish donning my lingerie.

One sticks out most of all.

Does he know? Has he known all along?

A knock at my door distracts me.

But that thought clings to the back of my mind, waiting for the perfect moment to seek an answer.

CHAPTER EIGHTEEN

Dexter and I wait, hidden from the rest of the party by trees, outside the door that led me into the garden my first morning here.

My life, I decide.

I'm definitely afraid for my life more than my heart.

If I am who I think, and he is who I think, then there isn't any control over my heart.

Not where he is concerned.

It appears loving him is inevitable; time, places, and circumstances are irrelevant.

But my life?

Simply being around him seems to have potential deadly consequences.

And here I stand in a strapless ivory wedding dress about to hitch myself to what might be a one-way ticket to doom.

I tremble from the thought.

"You can always back out," he murmurs, bending low so only I can hear him. "Turn around and go right back up those steps."

"The door doesn't open from the outside," I retort, my voice cracking. "Besides, I have to marry him."

He pulls me further away and uses a finger to tilt my chin up so he can look me in the face.

"You don't have to do anything. Would it suck to lose your diner? Yes. But it wouldn't be the end of the world."

"It's not about the diner." I take a deep breath and let it out slowly. "I'm not sure you'd believe what is it about even if I told you."

He looks at his watch. "You've got two minutes until that music cues the beginning of the next year of your life at the very least. Try me."

Two minutes.

I can't possibly sum up everything in that amount of time.

So I say something I know he will not interpret the way I mean it, for my comfort of knowing I voiced my thoughts when it all comes crashing around my head.

"What if loving him kills me?"

He laughs, leaning in to give me a kiss on the cheek under my veil, stating, "Oh hon, if you do end up loving him, I can assure you it will not kill you. And if anyone has ever claimed such a thing as true, they were turning a blind eye to their surrounding reality."

With that, the wedding march begins.

"Ready?" He holds his arm out, and I take it. "Smile, sweetheart. This is your day, no matter how it came about."

I force myself to relax.

And think about the surprise I have planned for Tobias when we're all alone.

The grin on my face is one-hundred percent real as I take the first step forward to what I now feel is my fate.

MOVING DOWN THE AISLE FEELS SURREAL.

I have never dreamed of getting married; never had a fantasy wedding I kept in mind. Not when I was a young child, nor a young adult.

Yet, I think if I had, this would have been it.

Perfect weather, a beautiful dress, beaming faces on either side, and a completely fuckable groom standing at the altar.

Yep, definitely.

The only thing that could've made it better was if my father and I had made amends, and he'd lived to attend the wedding.

But a girl can't have it all.

Nearing Tobias, the excitement I should've been feeling all along courses through me.

Tobias is wearing the light gray suit with the red tie at my request. The simple sight of him in the suit where this all began sets my body on fire.

I can't wait to be alone with him later.

The men wear the same, while the women wear red dresses.

To match, I wore a red sash around the waist, giving me the same pop of color as my groom.

Dexter 'gives me' to Tobias.

As he holds my hands, I try to focus on the ceremony and fail.

All I can think about is how naked we'll be in a very short time from now. I can't help but smile from behind my veil, which Tobias reciprocates along with a wink.

"Please repeat after me. I, Jocelyn Lunabella Bates, take thee, Tobias Alexander Giles-Blackburn…"

His eyes twinkle at the reminder of our first encounter, as if the suit wasn't enough, while I promise to love and cherish him.

Then, it's his turn.

"I, Tobias Alexander Giles-Blackburn, take thee, Jocelyn Lunabella Bates…"

Even though I expect the words, my heart still

squeezes in my chest as his eyes burn with desire into mine.

Because out of all the men in the world, this one is mine, whether or not I like it.

And as he slips the ring on my finger, I can't prevent a tear from escaping and sliding down my cheek.

Another one falls as we're pronounced husband and wife, Tobias lifting my veil to finalize our union with a kiss.

His smile softens as he uses the pad of his thumb to brush the tear away. His lips are gentle upon mine at first, almost admiring. When I wrap my arms around his neck, everyone cheers, and his mouth becomes firm, demanding.

He releases me and takes my hand to walk back down the aisle.

I keep a smile on my face even as the tears continue to stream, knowing everyone will assume they are tears of joy.

But I know we will end up loving each other.

And that the very act of doing so may be our ruin.

Perhaps even our deaths.

CHAPTER NINETEEN

THAT'S IT.

I'm a married woman.

Here we are hours after our wedding, back at his — our? — house and I can't believe it.

Tomorrow the real world will intervene.

The papers to pay off the diner and make it mine will be given to the lawyer.

An announcement of our marriage — along with a picture of us — will be released with enough information to keep people who are interested happy.

I laughed when he said that would happen; how I will go from being relatively unknown, to people being curious about me and wanting to know everything about the bride one exceedingly eligible bachelor chose, and proceeded to marry in relative secrecy.

The pregnancy rumors will definitely swirl.

As for me, well, they can dig all they want. I hope my lack of anything scandalous doesn't bore them to death.

I push all those thoughts aside as Tobias wraps his arms around my waist from behind and kisses my exposed shoulder.

"Hello, wife."

That is about the twentieth time today he's used the term. After the ceremony while answering questions, having our pictures taken, chatting during the reception, and even on the ride home, he simply referred to me as 'wife.' I don't know if he is training for an Olympic sport in it or what.

"When will you return to calling me by my name?" I turn in his arms. "Hmm, *husband?*"

He grins down at me before lowering his head and placing his lips on mine.

Weeks. It's been weeks since we've had sex thanks to his impromptu business trip. And I want sex. Badly.

But, I have a plan, and can't let him divert my attention.

I pull away before he can deepen the kiss and point across the room as his expression changes from horny to confused. He looks to see what I'm indicating, then turns back to me with one brow lifted.

"What's the chair for? You want tied up?"

"No." I shake my head, stepping back enough that he

lets me go. "It's for you. That is if you want the something special I've planned."

His expression remains the same as he shakes his head. "For me? You want to tie *me* to the chair? No way."

I hold up one of his ties. "Yes, way. And it's just your hands so you can't touch."

"What if I promise I won't?"

"Nope." I nod toward the chair. "Even if you will no doubt be able to get the tie off, I figure it will be a nice reminder to behave. Now take off your clothes and sit."

Tobias crosses his arms, the intense look he aims at me making me flush. "And if I don't? If I take you over my knee and spank you for telling me to 'sit' like a dog instead?"

Yes, please!

I take a step in his direction, unbuttoning his shirt while smiling up at him. "If you don't, well, I didn't see a sentence anywhere in the agreement saying I'm required to have sex with you — at all."

At that, he frowns. "That's cruel."

I laugh, mostly because I've never told him how much I *need* sex, and therefore, will never be able to go without. The weeks he wasn't here tortured me and I have no desire for an extended repeat. "You're the one being difficult. I'm trying to get you naked."

Going up on tiptoe, I brush my lips against his before stepping back. "I'll be right back. Be ready for me!"

After reaching the door, I glance back in time to see him pulling off his shirt.

Grinning, I head into the bathroom to prepare for ensuring Tobias has a wedding night he will never forget.

❧

Tobias sits naked in the chair facing the bed.

I shut the door behind me after re-entering, and his body tenses. He doesn't look my way as I walk closer, swiping the tie from atop the dresser before standing behind him. I squat down and, without me even saying a word, he places his hands around the back of the chair, one palm cupping the other hand. I tie him enough that he is deterred, but able to get himself out with a bit of effort.

I count on him getting free anyway, but he doesn't know that.

Grinning, I rise and walk around to stand in front of him.

He sucks in a breath at the sight of me, his cock instantly standing at attention.

I'm wearing thigh-high stockings, black pumps, and a teddy. A lacy, scrap of a thing, with a deep v-neck in the front and back that leads into a g-string. I've left my hair free, the ends brushing against the top of my ass.

The hunger on his face when his perusal leads to his eyes meeting mine at last nearly makes me toss my plan aside. His cock is begging for attention, and my pussy clenches at the thought of having him inside me. I know we will fuck all night long; it's been a long wait, and we will not stop until we're both sated.

But, for now, we are going to do things my way.

First up: teasing.

I say nothing while kneeling between his legs. When my body touches the chair, I rest my hands on his thighs and look up into his face. He watches me, eyes hooded, which flicker to life when I lick my lips.

Taking his cock in hand, I wrap my fingers around and squeeze, making him moan at the contact. I drop my eyes when he tilts his head back, lifting his hips to thrust into my palm. Licking around the head, then down the shaft, I move my hand up and down in a slow, steady rhythm meant to torture him. Occasionally squeezing, I go all the way to the base, stopping to worship the object of my affection with a kiss every few seconds.

And it is true regard because I love his cock. If I were a porn star named Goldilocks and had to choose between which of the three cocks in a gang bang would fuck me first, I would choose his hands down. Not too big, not too small, but just right.

His cock will give me so much pleasure tonight and has since the first night we met. Even then, there hadn't been an 'oh, no, how will that fit?' moment. Nope, he has the perfect cock, for me.

I don't take him in my mouth like I know he wants me to. Instead, I give a final kiss to the top and remove my hand, standing up once more. When he opens his eyes, I wink before turning and striding away. Grabbing the bag packed the previous evening, I bring it back over to the bed and start going through the contents.

"It's rude to start something then walk away." Amusement fills his words, making me smile as he inquires, "What're you doing over there?"

That's when I take out the toy and shove the bag to the side. Climbing onto the bed, I sit on the edge and hold it up for him.

His eyes widen at the sight of a pink vibrator. Nothing fancy, but with a bulbous head, a thin middle, and a white area on the bottom that holds the controls. It happens to be my favorite for-my-use only toy, and tonight, I'm going to give him an up close and personal demonstration for the hell of it.

Oh, who am I kidding?

I want to torture him by playing with myself in front of him and making him watch, unable to touch.

As a reminder, I glare at him. "If you try to get loose and join in, all the fun stops. Got it?"

I swear his eyes are on fire now, nodding at my words even as his cock twitches, no doubt at the thoughts going through his mind at what I'm about to do. I have a feeling he wishes he could spank me right now for talking to him that way, which makes this all the more delicious because I know he'll pay me back later.

Locking eyes with him, I use my empty hand to slip underneath one side of the teddy and cup my breast. Pinching my nipple between my thumb and forefinger, I moan in pleasure...and Tobias glares in response.

"I should be doing that." His voice is thick with lust. "Untie me."

Shaking my head, I continue to alternate between pinching and caressing. Putting the toy up to my mouth, I lick it, around and around, getting it nice and wet before sliding it under the fabric covering my pussy.

The toy moves smoothly, aided by the slickness along with the teddy not being tight enough to hinder its trail down until it slips between my lips. I rest it on my clit, then use my thumb to hit the key I know will set the toy to buzzing on the lowest level.

For a few minutes, I don't do anything else. I leave the toy there, teasing myself while using both hands to fondle my breasts, keeping the nipples peaked. Then, reaching down, I hold on to the toy while scooting back the tiniest bit, smiling at him seconds before I lie flat on my back and spread my legs.

"Oh god, Joce..." Need is evident in his every word. "You don't play fair."

Nope, I don't.

I can't articulate this, though, focused as I am on my

pleasure. I turn up the buzz a little as I move the tip, around, over, around my clit again. I've pushed the scrap covering me to the side, exposing every single moment of the show to his eyes. I can't see him, but there is no question I'm the center of his attention.

Shocking me, he does something I should've expected yet didn't.

He starts talking dirty.

"Fuck, look at you." He growls, voice low and exuding desire. "So wet. You're wishing my hard cock inside your tight, wet pussy, aren't you love?"

Yes!

I laugh, turning the toy higher as I move it lower, moaning in response. "No. Not at all."

"Liar." He chuckles, and I hear the chair creak. "You're in so much trouble when I'm free. That beautiful cunt deserves so much more than you're giving it right now."

"Does it?" Damn, I love teasing him. "And you think you're it, do you? How do you know my pussy missed you? Maybe I kept it more than happy."

"Happy? I'm sure you did." Another creak of the chair. I'm trying not to moan as tingles shoot through my arms and legs, stronger each time his beautiful, intense voice reaches my ears. "But ecstatic? Delirious? So pleased your body is exhausted and can't go another moment? No. You'll get that with me, and only with me. You and that gorgeous, glistening cunt will never be sated by anybody else but me."

A sob escapes, his statement doing something to me I can't make sense of in this moment, my orgasm ripping through me. My eyes slam shut as I yank the toy away, my pussy clenching as wave upon wave of pleasure leaves me gasping. When the tension passes, my feet slide off the bed, legs unable to stay up any longer.

"Stunning."

The awe in that word alone has me forcing myself up before I can examine why it makes the twist in my heart border on happy.

It's a good thing I put his chair so close; my wobbly legs don't have to carry me too far.

Placing my hands on his shoulders, I climb on to his lap, sliding my pussy down on his cock inch by agonizing inch.

His eyes sear into mine as he whispers, "Welcome to the best seat in the house, Joce."

I can't help it; I smile. A big, happy grin because the past few weeks without sex have been absolute torture.

Nothing more needs said as I lean forward and press my lips against his. They part under mine in an instant, our tongues tangling as we both moan in unison. I slide my arms around his neck and my hands into his hair, kissing him with every ounce of the pent up sexual frustration pulsing through me.

He fills me. Teasing, I do a Kegel, clenching around him; he thrusts in response, laughing into my mouth. Lifting up until the tip of his cock is in danger of falling out, I drag my lips away and look him directly in the eyes.

"You never told me why it's only a year."

He chuckles, raising his ass off the chair to tease us both. "You really want to talk about this right now?"

"Do you want to get off?"

He lowers himself back to the seat, sighing. "I'm not an ogre. A year is long enough."

"I see." I move down, both of us moaning as I settle completely, then rise again. "Long enough for what?"

I pause once more, and he growls — no doubt in frustration at my manipulation of this situation. But I want to know.

That's when he brings his arms around and grabs my hips, pushing them down as he lifts once more, plunging his cock deep inside. He holds me there, regarding me with amusement and lust.

"To get to know you. For you to get to know me." He raises me up before bringing my body back down again, eliciting a loud gasp from both of us. "I knew you wouldn't date me — you don't date anyone — so I used the situation to my advantage. You know it. I know it."

Before I can respond, he slides his hands up my sides, wrapping his arms around my torso to bring my body flush against his as he stands up in one swift movement. I cry out as I land on my back on the bed, his body covering mine as he takes control.

Just like I hoped he would.

Knew he would.

His lips trail down, taking a nipple into his mouth, sucking and nipping it through the fabric; I slip my hands into his hair and tug on it. He looks up at me, eyes glinting in the low light.

"Were you free the whole time?"

He grins. "You said if I tried to get loose *and* join in, you'd stop. You didn't say anything about getting loose and continuing to watch." He picks up the toy, smile turning wicked. "My turn."

Tugging my body to the edge of the bed, he stands between my legs and lifts them, my feet resting on his shoulders. They quiver — hell, I tremble with anticipation — as he uses one hand to guide his cock to me, sliding it up and down. I whimper, raising my hips to try and make him give me what I so desperately need right now.

Then, he pushes himself inside me with one long stroke. My eyes slam shut, and I moan; he lets out a groan of his own, gripping my hip with his now free hand to hold me still as he pauses. I hear the buzz of the toy seconds before it's against my clit, the hum mixing with our own sounds of pleasure as he moves, stroking in and out while moving the toy against me as I had myself. As if he'd memorized what had pleased me just moments ago.

"Oh god. To—" I don't even get the words out as I come again, my body at his complete mercy.

"Mmm." He continues his long, slow thrusts, keeping the toy against me while putting it on the highest level. "You're so fucking sexy. One more time, love. I love it when you clench around me."

I can't help it; the toy is so high my body has no choice except to give him what he wants. I wail as it rips through me once more. I barely register him dropping the toy and holding both hips. He speeds up, and within seconds, he lets out a groan and collapses on top of me.

One thought crosses my mind while I lie there in heaven.

Sex with him is the best I've ever had and probably will ever have again.

CHAPTER TWENTY

I'M COLD AND HUNGRY.

Where's my mommy? Or my daddy.

I woke up after taking my nap like a good girl just like my mommy said I was, and now I can't find them.

I cried and cried.

Why haven't they come back?

I'm only three.

That's what my mommy says when her friends come around, and they get mad at me.

"She's only three. She doesn't know any better."

I feel so tired now.

My tummy hurts.

I'm afraid to go outside. Mommy says there's no reason to go outside. That people are mean.

I don't like mean people.

But I'm so hungry.

I open the door. It's heavy, but I need to find my mommy.

She's so mean. So's my daddy.

Where did they go?

I hate them for not taking me.

I love them.

I can't see. It's so bright.

"Mommy! Daddy!" I'm scared. I yell over and over. "Mommy! Daddy! I'm scared!"

People walk by and stare me. Then, keep walking.

Not my mommy. Not my daddy.

But they look so nice.

I'm hungry. Maybe they have food.

"Help me!" I run up to them. "Mommy and daddy left me alone. I'm hungry."

They stare down at me, frowning.

Why are they mad at me? What did I do?

Then the pretty lady smiles.

"Sweetie, why don't you come with us? We will find your mommy and daddy."

"Caroline, we can't just take the girl off the street!" The man has a loud voice, but it doesn't scare me. "Let me call the cops."

He has a nice voice. I decide I like these people.

I take the lady's hand while the guy calls cops, whoever they are.

Why did mommy say people are mean?

I think I like them more than my mommy and daddy.

"Joce?"

Tobias is stroking my cheek.

I swat his hand away, opening my eyes to find the room still dark. "Why is your hand wet?"

"You're crying."

"What? No, I'm not. I was sleeping." I bring my hand up to my face and wipe the wetness away. "Don't mess with me."

I can't see his face, but I know he's close.

Then, near my ear, as he takes the lobe in his mouth and nips it. "I'm not. You were crying in your sleep; your sniffles woke me up."

"I—" Not sure I can tell him, I turn on my side and face away. "I'm sorry."

"Don't be." He wraps his body around me from behind, resting his chin on my upper arm. "Instead, tell me what's wrong."

H won't leave me alone until I give in. Sighing, I tell him what he wants to know. "A dream. At least, I think it was just a dream. It was weird, though."

"Hmm?"

"There was a little girl. She wakes up all alone, her parents gone. She waits, but they don't come back. So, she goes outside even though she's scared and runs to this couple on the sidewalk. The whole time she's hungry and thinking how her mommy always said all the people outside are mean; that she shouldn't go out there."

I pause, and Tobias gives my arm a reassuring squeeze.

"That is sad."

I shrug his hand off, and he removes it as I turn over toward him, making sure our bodies touch.

"That's not the worst part." I place a hand on his shoulder and scoot close, resting my head in the crook of his neck as his free arm wraps around me. "T-the woman takes her hand and says they will help her find her parents, while the man says that he will call the cops. T-the man was my father; the woman my mother. A-and...," I take a shuddering breath. "the little girl was me."

I'm so close to his face that his breath catches against my cheek.

"Your mother and father? As in the ones who left the little girl alone?"

"No." A tear slips down my cheek. "My parents — Derrick and Caroline."

I drag myself out of his arms and sit up, reaching over to turn on the light.

Tobias' brow is furrowed in confusion, trying to understand what I'm saying to him. And as another tear slides down my cheek, my lower lip wobbles as I explain.

"My f-father...he was just trying to protect me. He

didn't want me to know and never planned to tell me." His eyes widen, but I don't stop. I can't now after that dream. "We g-got into a fight before I went off to c-college. He told me they adopted me. He said both of them loved me from the moment I put my hands in theirs. I had no idea..."

I can't even finish the sentence. I know it was no dream, but a memory that had lurked inside my mind until tonight.

Tobias pulls me back into his embrace and wraps his arms around me as the tears I bottled up inside me years ago finally find their way out. His arms tighten as he lifts one hand and begins to stroke my hair.

After a few moments, as the tears slow, he asks, "How did your mom...pass? Your father never said."

"Um." I swipe at my eyes, trying to wipe the tears away, and failing. "I was twelve. She...she died in a fire at her work, along with a few co-workers. They were trapped and couldn't escape in time."

"Fuck's sake."

I lift my head and look up into his face. "Why don't you know this? I know you did a background on me; that's the only way you could've figured out I don't have any family."

"No." He runs a hand through his hair, frowning. "I didn't delve that far. I only knew she wasn't alive, not how she died."

I nod, then bring my eyes back to his as mine fill with

tears once more. "I loved them. I never got the chance to tell him 'sorry' — all I could see was my own anger at them keeping such a secret from me. And what for? They took me in; they loved me. He died thinking...thinking I hated him. That was the last thing I ever said to him before I left for college."

"That's not true." Tobias cups my face in his palm, smiling. "He talked about you all the time. He was very proud of you. He never told me why you two weren't talking, but his love for you...it shown in his eyes, in the grin on his face every time he said your name. You were his joy."

His words don't take away the pain; after all, I'll never get to hear my father says those words. I'll never get to say sorry for the way I acted either. But a little of the vice around my heart, and the anger at myself I've been carrying around dissipates a bit at knowing my father loved me even when I hadn't deserved it.

Also, I feel lucky that Tobias is the one who can give me such important information. I return his touch, stroking his cheek with my thumb as I lean in and kiss him on the mouth.

"Thank you. I haven't said it before now but thank you for being there for him. For being his friend. For telling me that. I wouldn't have blamed him for being mad—"

Cutting off my words with a finger over the lips, he grins and shakes his head at my statement. "It was my pleasure. I loved your father. And if you want to thank me..." He slides his hand down until it skims my breast, cupping it and squeezing gently. "How about you show me instead?"

I roll my eyes. "You're such a man."

"You love it."

I don't reply, moving to turn the light off before turning back into his arms.

A place that is starting to feel more than temporary and more like where I belong forever.

His lips descend on mine before that thought can make me panic, our mutual pleasure becoming the main focus.

"BRYNJA IS DEAD?"

I swallow the bile rising in my throat, frozen where I stand, as the man I hate answers.

"Yes. I had to kill her. She would have told them the plans she heard. That cannot happen."

A loud thump — I assume Brynja's father hit his hand against the desk — and then he says, "You must continue with your plans to get rid of her. She mustn't marry my son. Though I do not know how we will cover up two deaths so close to one another."

"We do not announce your daughter's death. Tell them

she ran away; they shan't know the difference. She has always been a wild one."

"'Tis a relief I have other daughters I am able to marry off." Her father laughs as the sickness rises from my chest. "A man must have ways to pay his debts, after all. Get gone and do your duties."

Foot falls head toward the door. I back away, panic rising as my eyes dart around, searching for the closest place to hide.

He mustn't find me.

I know it is me they were speaking about.

I am in love with his son.

And they have somehow discovered our plans to marry.

Opening a door I know to be a closet, I close it and hunch down, praying he doesn't realize someone has been listening. I hear him pause outside the door, and my breath catches.

Brynja is dead.

He killed her.

My love will be devastated.

His uncle killed his sister and now, he planned to kill his nephew's fiancé.

As his footsteps retreat, I wait a few moments before leaving the small space, running for my life.

I must warn him, and we must make a run for it tonight.

Before it is too late.

CHAPTER TWENTY-ONE

I JERK AWAKE, HAND COVERING THE POUNDING OF MY heart, as I take in my surroundings.

The brightness of the sun streams through the window announcing the morning's arrival.

Which tells me one very important thing, overshadowing the dream: I'm late for work.

"Shit!" Turning my head to the left, I lift my right arm and poke him in the side. "Let me up. I'm late!"

"Mmm, no." He mumbles this while pulling my body closer to his, trapping my left arm between us. "Shh. Go back to sleep."

"You can sleep all you like; I have to work."

"It's Saturday." He opens one eye and tugs me even closer. "Plus, you took this weekend off remember? We're going to move your stuff today."

Ah, yes, that's correct. "Right," is what I say out loud.

I forgot about my decision to move in with him after we were married rather than before. With him being gone those weeks prior to the wedding anyway, everything had worked out perfectly.

His hand starts roaming as I let go of the fear about being late for work, only to have the dream find its way back in. I turn my face, finding him with his eyes closed once more even as his hand continues to caress my body, the strokes almost rhythmic in their motion. Down my abdomen, over to the left, fingertips skimming back to near my breasts, back down, to the right and up.

It's oddly comforting.

What is even more strange is the utter contentment I feel while lying here.

I don't really dwell on things. It's not in my nature and never has been. I decided I was in and here I am. Had I liked the inevitability of my situation? No, but I accepted it and don't question how I feel anymore, or why he wanted to marry me, or if our marriage will even be successful.

The only questions that remain, for me, are if he feels the same connection to me as I do with him.

If he has dreams.

If he knows more than he lets on.

"What're you thinking about?"

His words interrupt my thoughts, his eyes still closed.

How does he do that?

He chuckles, opening his eyes to stare into mine. "Your

body tenses when you're deep in thought. That's how I do it."

My face heats while realizing I've asked that out loud.

"Joce." His snicker turns into a full blown laugh. He brings a hand to my face, cupping it as his thumb strokes my cheek, eyes twinkling with amusement. "You're so beautiful when you blush like that. Tell me what you were thinking about."

I lick my lips, mouth going dry at the fear of telling him about the dreams, and having him end up laughing at me. His eyes drop, darkening. My breath hitches as his cock hardens even more against my leg, begging for my attention. I turn in his arms, bringing my arms up to wrap around his neck as he smiles down at me.

"On second thought..." He lowers his head, his mouth capturing mine for a second before he pulls away enough to whisper, "we'll talk after I have my early morning snack. I'm starving."

Before I can respond, he rolls me over and under him, pulling the comforter over both our heads with a naughty chuckle.

Encasing us in darkness and for the moment, saving me from potentially looking like a crazy person.

But I know I'll have to tell him soon because an instinct I can't explain is telling me these dreams are more than just a distant memory.

Our early morning snack turns into two, after which we both promptly fall back to sleep.

Making us late to start moving things from the apartment to the house.

We shower and dress quickly; when we finally arrive, Iris and Dexter are sitting in the living room.

"Hey! Sorry, we're so late—"

My apology is interrupted as Iris jumps up and envelops me in a tight hug, squeezing all the breath out of me. "Don't be sorry! We both knew you two would probably be late, didn't we Dexter?"

She tosses him a wink as she releases me.

Dexter runs a hand through his hair, looking up at me with a grin. "Yep. I'm still waking up myself. Iris and I stayed up way too late drinking. Celebrating you getting married, of course."

Behind me, Tobias laughs, and I join in. Iris rolls her eyes and sits back on the couch.

Taking his hand in mine, I smile up at him, feeling a little awkward and a bit sad. This is the end of one part of my life and the beginning of another.

I must be making a face because Tobias squeezes my hand reassuringly.

Tightening my hand in response, I return my focus back to my friends. "Ready to help me get these boxes out of here?"

Dexter jumps up, pulling Iris with him, both turning to face me. "Anything for you, Joce."

That's when the room blurs around me, and I slam my eyes shut.

I'm running through the woods.

I must find my love. If they find me first, they shall kill me just like they killed his sister.

I must tell him they killed his sister.

My eyes blur as I stumble toward our meeting place. I know he is waiting for me.

We never meet at the same time, knowing such predictability could end up getting us killed.

Today.

Today is the day when we run.

We have no choice.

The sun is going down, but I know my way.

A path I have traveled many times, and one I know after tonight, I shall never travel again.

I never see it coming.

The dark seeps in and I am grabbed from behind, my mouth covered, my scream silenced before it ever has a chance to escape.

A sweet smell fills my senses, and as the darkness from the sky becomes the darkness in my mind, I register one final thought.

Tonight is the night I die.

"Joce! Wake up, right fucking now!" Tobias taps my cheek as I moan. "That's it. Open your eyes, love."

My eyelids heavy, I drag them open to do as he commands, discovering his total domination of the space around me. He's placed his body over mine as I lie on the carpet, and is resting on both elbows, his face mere inches from mine.

"I'm taking you to the hospital." His voice is tight, his jaw clenching as his eyes fill with worry. "This is the second time—"

"No." Taking a deep breath, I let it out slowly, then frown. "The hospital won't be able to do anything; I'm not sick."

"Not sick? You're passing out randomly. You don't sleep like you should." His voice rises. "You wake up gasping for air."

I can't see Iris or Dexter, but they are murmuring somewhere behind me. My chest constricts, the worry about what they'll all think like a vise around my heart. "I..."

His face softens even as his eyes blaze. "If you're not sick, then what's the problem, Joce? Are you narcoleptic?"

The unexpected question elicits a bark of laughter from me and I shake my head. "I wish I was. Let me sit up."

He moves out of the way and offers a hand. Once I'm sitting up, he scoots close to me, putting his arm around my shoulders. Then, Iris and Dexter sit down facing me; all of them look at me expectedly.

Their stares are too much for me, and I drop my eyes into my lap. "I've been having dreams." I look up, catching Tobias' eyes with my own and give him a weak smile. "Beyond the dream I told you about last night. I started having them weeks ago, and sometimes, they happen when I'm awake."

"Suppressed memories?"

"I don't know; I don't think so. The one I told you about yes. These others...they involve different...times."

"Wait," Dexter says, causing me to drag my eyes away from a wide-eyed Tobias to look at him. "What dream did you tell him about? I'm lost."

And here I am, about to tell one lifetime friend, and another from college who has become like a brother, the real reason my father and I stopped speaking. I move my eyes to focus on Iris as the words spring forth.

"I had a dream that when I was three, I woke up from a nap to find my parents gone. I was afraid to go outside, but eventually, I did. And I ran to a couple, asking them to help me. I told them I was hungry and that my mommy and daddy left me alone. I put my hand in the woman's after she said they would help me, while the man told her he'd have to call the police." I take a deep breath, then close my eyes briefly before opening them, whispering, "They were my parents. I was — no, I *am* adopted."

Iris glares at me, her eyes filling with tears. "How could you keep such a thing from me? You told me he was angry at you going so far away for school with me!"

"I wasn't ready to talk about it!" My own eyes grow blurry through my tears. Tobias takes my hand in his, but all my focus and attention remains on Iris, wanting her to understand. "He never told me any details. Just that they adopted me. I don't even know if that dream is true or what really happened. All I know is, my father told me at age eighteen. I felt betrayed and told him I hated him for keeping such a thing from me my whole life. He *died*, and those were my last words to him!"

With that, Iris leans forward, crawling the small distance to where I'm sitting and pulls me into a tight hug.

"I'm sorry." I hug her back. "Nobody is more mad at me than I am at myself, but I should've told you—"

She shakes her head, sniffling as she releases me and leans back. "It's okay, I understand. Tell us about these other dreams..."

Giving her a smile, she resumes her seat next to Dexter as I tell them all about what I've dreamt, one by one. I don't go into too many details, mostly citing the important parts. When I finish, Iris and Dexter are staring at me open mouthed; Tobias, on the other hand, looks thoughtful, his gaze intense and locked on me.

"They're just dreams, right?" I give a hopeful look to

all three of them. "I mean, yeah, they are inconvenient, but..."

Tobias shakes his head. "The most recent one; you were awake when it came on. People dream during REM. You weren't...well, *asleep* long enough for that to happen this time or the time at my parents' house."

I release his hand and stand up. "Why should I believe they are anything else?" Walking over, I pick up a box, heading toward the door with a pointed glance at Tobias. "Shall we?"

They must all see it as the end of our discussion because they help me get the boxes into the car, no more mention of dreams. When we're done, I tell Iris and Dexter I'll see them sometime during the week for dinner, and we hug goodbye.

But, as we drive away from the apartment, I stare at Tobias because we're heading in the wrong direction. "Where are we going?"

"Who did it?" He tosses me a look before watching the road again. "In the last one, who was it?"

His sudden question catches me off guard. "I—I don't know."

"You said you were running, that *they* were going to kill you. Who were 'they,' Joce? Do you know?"

"Y—yeah, actually, I do." I hadn't revealed who in the dream had talked about killing the girl, figuring they didn't need to hear the grisly details but since he's asking, I might as well. "The father told the uncle to do it. So, I guess he did. He had to've killed...me."

I feel strange saying the man killed me. *It was just a dream!* Yet, Tobias is shaking his head.

"What?"

His hands tighten on the wheel. "I'll tell you when we get to my parents."

"No. Tell me now." I rest my hand on his leg. "Why are you shaking your head no?"

When he says nothing, I follow suit, glaring at him in hopes he'll relent.

After a few drawn out minutes, he sighs and takes my hand in his, lifting it up to his lips. Giving them a quick kiss, he returns my hand to my lap before gazing at the road once more. What he says next has my blood running cold.

"They didn't kill you, Joce. It was my uncle Artemis who grabbed you in those woods, and once he had you sufficiently drugged—" He sucks in a breath but doesn't look at me. "He convinced you we were cursed, and the only way to break the spell was to kill me."

CHAPTER TWENTY-TWO

I'M NOT SPEECHLESS.

I probably should be. Instead, I'm fuming.

"You know? Why wouldn't you tell me in the first place?"

He scoffs at that, throwing me an 'are you serious' look. "There is no way you would've accepted this strange man sitting in your diner coming up to you and saying, 'gee, I don't know if you know this or not, but I'm your soulmate, and we've lived six previous lives together. Give me another chance?'"

Okay, he has a point.

And I'm curious enough at this point to push aside the thought that even having this conversation makes me feel insane, and figure out what the hell is going on.

Seriously... six previous lives?

"Why would the dreams start after I met you and not before?"

"I don't know." He shrugs, tossing me a rueful smile. "Truth is, you've never remembered before."

This is getting more interesting by the second.

"You found me. You chased after me. You deliberately used my situation to get me to marry you." My thoughts are going a mile a minute, finding their way out of my mouth as I try to understand. "Did you plan it all, even befriending my father? Wait, did my father know? If I've never remembered before, how did we end up together each time? Do you have the dreams too? Did you—"

"Hold on." He cuts in, grabbing my hand and squeezing gently. "I have always known. Each time I would die, when I was born again I grew up knowing all about our history. I don't know *why* you didn't remember each time, but I've always believed it has to do with us having to work to break the curse."

He shrugs. "This is the first time you've had any notion of our past, which is strange all on its own. And no, your father didn't know. As a matter of fact, I was shocked to discover that you were, well, you."

For some reason, that statement bothers me more than it should. "Why?"

"First, neither of us look the same as we always did. We don't come back with the same looks; the fact you saw this face in your dreams is interesting, but the only thing either of us has kept is the color of our hair and eyes." I nod when he throws a glance my way, then watches the road once more as he continues. "And second, in all the lives we've lived, you were always the rich one. You came from a rich family, which is why they were trying to keep us apart in the first place. You've got the hair and eyes, but your family wasn't rich."

This is fascinating, so I ask the next obvious question.

"What about your family? You guys aren't poor. Did our positions in life switch perhaps?"

He laughs, shaking his head. "Oh, we were poor for a long time. Any improvements to the farm are thanks to me — not that I ever mention it. We were on the brink of losing it for a while, barely able to keep up."

"But you're rich now, so maybe that's all that matters. And, after all, I was adopted."

"I've thought about that." He turns onto the road that will have us at his parents in five minutes, then continues. "But we don't have enough details. The dream has you running out of a house in which you were left alone. We don't know where this house was or who your real parents were. But you were three and ended up being adopted, which can only lead me to conclude that nobody ever stepped forward to claim you. Don't you believe if your parents were rich, that somebody wouldn't have stepped forward and said, 'Hey, I know that kid.'?"

I'm not really sure what to make of this. I do, however,

have one last lingering question. "How did you know I was, well, me?" I copy his earlier statement, and he chuckles.

"I didn't know when I met your father. Like I said, we spent a lot of time together, but neither of us had a clue, until that day we went fishing and he described you."

He pulls into his family's driveway. "When I saw you in that diner once I came back, I recognized you. There was no doubt." Once he parks the car and shuts it off, he turns to me and takes both my hands in his. "You were different than I'm used to, though. Here you were...this shy, distant, and to be honest, a bit dowdy woman, when you've always been a vivacious, fiery, and formidable woman. A warrior to be reckoned with who died for me. Many times, apparently."

Lifting my hands to his lips, he kisses each of them before locking his intense gaze on me. "Then I met you as Luna — deliberately, so you're aware — and saw that you're exquisite as you've always been. You're beautiful inside and out; stubborn, devoted, and a gigantic — albeit adorable — pain in my ass."

"Wow, I almost liked you there for a second." The words have no heat, a smile stealing over my face at his compliments. Nodding at the house, I lift a brow, inquiring, "So...why are we here, exactly?"

"You'll see." He gives me a quick kiss on the mouth and releases my hands. "Let's go."

As he gets out of the car and I exit out my door, I have the sudden feeling that what I've learned is merely the beginning.

And I don't know whether I'm more intrigued...or terrified.

But when he takes my hand once more and leads me to the front door, I know one thing for sure: I'm one very lucky woman to have him.

I just hope I can love him like he deserves.

☙❧

RANDOLF IS THE FIRST TO SEE US ENTER THE HOUSE.

"Mom! Dad! Munchkin and his girl—wife are here!" He shoots me a smile. "Sorry, I still can't believe this idiot actually married someone."

I don't know what to say to that, so I laugh at his use of my joke nickname for Tobias, who rolls his eyes. "Ran, tell Mom, Dad and Breena to meet us in the living room. You can handle that, right?"

He doesn't wait for an answer before leading me away.

We aren't in the living room long when they all walk in. Sven and Liv are beaming, while Randolf and Breena both look tortured. Tobias stands up to hug his mother and father, while Breena goes to stand near the window and Randolf takes a seat in a nearby chair.

As they sit down, his mother speaks first. "We weren't expecting you."

Tobias continues to hold my hand as we sit next to each other on the sofa. He clasps it tightly as he announces, "She knows."

In an instant, all eyes are on me.

The room is pretty damn silent. I shift in my chair, looking at them one by one.

When they land on Randolf, he leans forward and smiles. "It's about damn time."

I don't get a chance to ask what the hell that means because Breena pipes in, "Why isn't she crying hysterically like she always does?" Then she laughs when I give her a confused look. "I'm just kidding. You've never been told before."

"I didn't tell her."

It's nearly comical, the way their eyes widen as they go back and forth between Tobias and me, trying to figure out what the hell is going on. Which is fine with me because I'm quite lost myself. However, I get the feeling that Tobias is having a ball right now, so I decide to fill them in.

"I remembered," I say, using air quotes. "Or, rather, they've mostly arrived in the form of dreams. For a few weeks now."

Filling them in as I had my friends earlier, they go from confused to nodding their heads by the end. But before they can comment or ask me questions, I fix my gaze on Breena.

"The girls. Their names. Was it deliberate?"

She nods, walking closer until she's standing next to Randolf, then sits on the arm of the chair. "When I found out it was twins, I was so excited. I thought I'd have a little boy and girl, especially since..." She pauses, biting her lip, and her eyes filling with tears. "Especially since, for some reason, Tobias and I weren't twins this time."

Dazed by this revelation, I turn to Tobias. "Twins?"

"Everything is messed up." He looks away from me to his sister. "Jocelyn has informed me that in the life she killed me..." He pauses, and I wince, meeting Breena's eyes as he proceeds, "you were killed by our uncle after you overheard his and our father's plot to kill her."

Breena pales at his words.

I frown at her. "You didn't know?"

Randolf puts his arm around her while she shakes her head. "No. I never saw their face. We wondered who could've—but we should've known. He had you kill Tobias; it's so obvious now."

"But why? He was ordered to get rid of me, not his—"

My statement is cut short, my hands gripping Tobias' arm as a sudden shot of pain through my head has me closing my eyes.

I'm screaming.

Blood. There is blood everywhere.

My loves eyes are empty, wide open and lifeless, his last breath drawn at my own hand.

It was the only way, that's what he said. He said we were cursed and the only way to break it was to kill him.

Only I do not know why that matters.

My heart is empty, frozen forever at the look of betrayal in his eyes as I struck true with the knife, straight to his heart.

Love.

What do I know of love?

My head hurts.

Screaming. Why am I screaming?

Why do I feel on fire?

I close my eyes, crouching down to the ground as I drop the knife, covering my head with my hands.

Squeezing.

Why won't it stop?

The pain. It hurts.

He's pulling my hair.

"Release me!"

My eyes meet his — my love's uncle — and find them full of hatred.

It matters not he's a handsome man.

For his soul is ugly.

My vision blurs as he drugs me again, holding me down as I scream louder and louder into the empty woods that shall never betray secrets.

It's cold.

My screams cease, the calm in my brain matching the outside world, now silent.

"You're mine," he whispers into my ear, confusing me as his tone is that of a lover. "And I shall make you see it's as you were meant to be."

No! *My brain is screaming, but I cannot speak any longer.*

I am languid; frozen.

And his kindness doesn't last.

For he drags me by my hair, through the snow, toward the cottage I know is nearby.

I am not afraid.

For now, I feel nothing.

And I never shall again.

I am sitting in Tobias' lap when I awake, cradled in his arms as I weep into his neck.

"He w-wanted me," I stutter through my tears. "Do you know where...?"

"No." He understands what I've left unspoken. "My father was born an only child this time."

"And he doesn't want to kill me?"

I expect a lot of reactions to my question, but not one of them involves them all laughing, which they do.

"I let you get married this time, didn't I?" Sven's chuckling voice breaks in through the laughter. "Not all of us are doomed to repeat the mistakes we've made in the past."

I sit up, facing him while wiping the tears from my eyes. "He never came back, did he?"

Sven shakes his head. "No. I sent people out to search for my son and found him dead. You and my brother were nowhere to be found, and never seen again."

"You thought we ran away together, didn't you?" My words are calm even as I feel like puking. "You would've had no idea..."

"Well." He smiles at me. "My son informed me that wasn't what happened years ago. We've been looking for you ever since. I'd say out of all of us, you're the one in the most danger. You need protected."

My eyes widen. "You think he'll come after me?"

"We don't know." Tobias answers this time. "But we have no way of knowing who he is this time. We all have to stay alert, be on guard."

"This is insane."

And it is. I don't know why I'm sitting here, believing this is all true, but I know this is the truth. I never ignore my instincts so I won't start now. But it doesn't mean I'm not kind of freaked out.

Because I am. A lot.

Tobias pulls me close, hugging me once more. "Don't worry. I won't let anyone hurt you."

"Isn't that what the hero always says to the heroine in romance novels right before she's kidnapped?"

His family laughs again, the tension easing just a little. I relax into his arms, trusting that protecting me is exactly what he plans to do.

Then, the doorbell rings.

CHAPTER TWENTY-THREE

SVEN ANSWERS THE DOOR AND SOON AFTER THE introductions, me and Tobias are sitting with his lawyer, Brandon Cain, inside his parents' study.

I'm not sure I like this man.

Not that the guy is slimy.

On the contrary, he seems pretty smart, as well as being very charming. I estimate him as around forty with his good looks, full head of dark blond hair and green eyes. His manner is very straightforward, his eyes rarely straying from Tobias' face as he goes over the prenuptial papers one final time.

He also sits behind the desk as if owns it.

Not doing anything to make me suspicious. Not staring at me as if fascinated, something I imagine someone who's obsessed with me and has been for six lifetimes, would very likely do.

Besides, Tobias wouldn't hire someone without fully vetting them, of that I'm sure.

I know there is no reason for my uneasiness except perhaps the conversation his family and I had right before this man's arrival.

Recognizing I'm projecting my fear of an unknown assailant onto this man unfairly, I relax into the chair and focus my attention on their conversation.

"Mrs.—" Mr. Cain smiles at me, his eyes meeting mine for the first time since he walked in. "Excuse me. What would you prefer to be called?"

Tobias informed me previously that he hired Mr. Cain — who specializes in several niche areas — when he started his business six years ago, keeping him on retainer for many of his legal needs. He seems very competent, his question firm and respectful in tone.

Since Tobias had apparently sent him a message to visit us here after our unexpected detour, I keep my tone the same and flash him a self-conscious smile. "Please, call me Jocelyn."

I haven't decided whether to change my name or not, but chances are I won't, at least professionally. However, Tobias and I haven't discussed it, and I don't see it as of any importance at this point.

He inclines his head. "Jocelyn, it is. Now," he says, looking up at me with a serious expression. "You agreed to the terms and signed these papers of your own free will, after seeking private counsel of your own?"

"Yes."

The terms are actually quite generous.

The year is only the initial term. It means I spend a year as his wife, and once that year has passed, the diner is mine free and clear. After that, for every year we stay married, I am entitled to a certain sum of money; any children include an extra amount along with provisions for the future care and education of each one of them.

Amounts that blew my mind, and even though children have been nowhere on my radar, the fact such things were thought of really makes me respect Tobias even more. He's thought of everything, and for once, it's nice not to have to worry.

Whether we stay married or not, I am set in all the ways that count: I'll have my diner.

Of course, I have no intention of leaving him — not after everything I've learned — nor do I believe he'll leave me, but I'm practical.

Shit happens.

That's one fact of life I never ignore, and I can't predict the future.

I would rather be safe than sorry any day.

"It's settled then." He gathers up his papers, pushing back his chair to stand up, then puts the papers into his briefcase as he speaks to Tobias. "If you need anything else, you know where to find me."

With that, he grins and pulls a newspaper out, holding it out to me. "Congratulations to both of you, by the way."

I glance down at the paper, only to gasp and remove it from his grasp.

Our wedding announcement is front page news.

"Oh! I didn't expect..."

Mr. Cain quietly exits the room while I peruse the article.

A picture of us, taken at the small reception, was used. We sat at the table with our arms hooked around one another, about to sip champagne, only to turn to the camera as we smiled brightly. My hair was down, face flush, lips rosy from his random and deep kisses, while Tobias looked as meticulous as always.

"It's the perfect picture," I whisper, turning my face to look at him, smiling. "Thank you."

He insisted he should be the one to choose the picture, especially when I declared I didn't care one way or another — I knew it was necessary, but I wasn't looking forward to the attention being his wife would get me.

I know I can't ignore it forever, but for now, I want to simply pretend it won't ever exist.

At least for another day or two.

Folding the paper and placing it on the desk, I stand up

and turn to him, popping one of the buttons on my shirt free.

"You should lock the door."

He does exactly that, then turns back to me and pounces.

His arms circle my waist, tugging me against him as he closes them around me, one hand sliding up my back and into my hair. He removes the clip, my hair falling from the chignon down my back, before wrapping the locks — still damp from my shower and rushed morning — around his hand and tugging, exposing my neck.

My body responds in an instant. My nipples go taut, poking through my thin bra as they beg for attention while delicious anticipation dances down my spine. He places a kiss by my ear, sending tingles through me; the scratch of his five o'clock shadow against my skin merely adding to the exquisite sensations.

Taking the lobe into his mouth, he nips it, coaxing a hiss of surprise from me before he sucks on it, soothing the hurt away as if it never occurred.

"You're welcome."

With those words, he slides his free arm down to my jean-clad ass, centering his hand as he holds me firmly, lifting up. I put my legs around him instinctively, fusing our mouths with a laugh. Taking a few steps forward, he sits me on top of the desk, stepping close.

I tighten my legs around him, unwilling to let him go.

Even as I wrap my arms around his neck and deepen our kiss, I know we shouldn't do this here. We should at least go to his room, the one we stayed in during our last visit. Before I decide whether or not to stop this, he pulls away and gazes down at me.

Removing his hands from me, he slides a hand inside my blouse, the material nothing against the force of his hand. His fingers slip into the cup of my bra, eliciting a gasp from me at the sweet mix of pleasure and pain as he pinches my nipple between two digits. Moving my arms to where I'm gripping his shoulders, I let my head tilt back a little and close my eyes, wanting nothing more than for him to keep going and never stop.

My desire isn't granted.

"You're insatiable." When he removes his hand, I lift my head and open my eyes to find him staring down at me with a wicked grin. "I fucking love it."

He cups my face in his hand, caressing my kiss swollen lips with the pad of his thumb. "You do nothing except look at me with those gorgeous eyes of yours and my cock is ready to go. If I could, I'd keep you in bed all day long; you were made for fucking. Made for me."

I suck in a breath, his possessive words belying the fire in his eyes. I don't even know what to say in reply, but I don't get the chance to reply even if I wanted it.

"You belong with me. *To* me. I've waited lifetimes to have you to myself, and I'm never letting you go." He leans in, possessing my mouth for a few moments with a ferocity that steals my breath away — a first for me — then he pulls back, wrapping me in his arms. "I'll protect you with everything I have; there isn't anything or anyone in this world worth losing you over. You're *mine* because I fucking say so, and no curse will keep me from the woman I love."

The unexpected declaration catches me off guard, my heart thumping hard.

"You—you can't fucking say that!"

His eyes glint with amusement as I try to push him away and am unsuccessful. "Can't say what? That I love you?" He touches my nose with his and laughs, low and filled with delight, his breath mingling with mine. "I love you, Joce. Now. Then. When you died for me. And even when you stabbed me through the heart. The heart that beat for you and still only beats for you."

My eyes fill with tears, my chest with sudden anger. "Stop!" I smack at his shoulders. "Let me go. Now!"

Tobias lets me go easily, stepping back, his lips still quirked in amusement. "Too soon, babe?"

"Fuck you." I glare at him, my hands shaking as I button my shirt up. "You don't play fair."

"You're damn right I don't." His mirth slips into a full-fledged grin. "You'll get used to it." He moves between my legs once more, smirking. "And if that fucker, whoever he is, thinks he'll get anywhere near you, he'll have another thing coming."

I look away, ignoring him and his declaration with the only weapon left in my emotional arsenal: silence.

Moving his mouth next to my ear and his hands to hold my waist lightly, he says in a soft tone, "Don't be angry, Joce. Six lifetimes — seven if you count this one — where I've loved and lost you. All I can tell you is how I feel, so you never have to guess where I stand. I want you. For now and for always. I know you don't know how you feel about me and that you're conflicted. But I'm here, and I'll wait."

A tear slips out at his sweet words, calling to me somewhere deep inside; a place I had no idea existed until now. A place I'm not ready to examine, for many reasons I'm sure can't be voiced aloud to myself at this point, let alone to him.

"Don't cry." He turns my face to his, locking his gaze with mine. Using his thumbs to brush away the evidence of feelings I can't cope with, he brushes his lips against mine. "After all, I have every intention of fucking you senseless when we get home."

Unable to resist, a laugh escapes me, and he smiles against my mouth.

A few minutes later, we're on our way so he can fulfill his promise to me.

Even though I know sex won't get his words off my mind.

The only thing that will do that is me figuring out how I feel.

Which means it's time for a talk with my two best friends; the only two people in the world who know me better than anyone else.

CHAPTER TWENTY-FOUR

I thought a return to normalcy would be just what I needed and that was wrong.

It's Monday morning. I'm sitting in my office, going over the paperwork done over the weekend, when Molly walks in.

"Your *husband* is here." Her cheerful emphasis on the word has me glaring at her after looking up from my task. "And he brought a friend. A gorgeous, huge man who looks like he can break me in two simply by looking at me hard enough."

"I'm sure you're exaggerating this friend's attributes." Standing up, I head toward and out the door, Molly on my heels. "As for Tobias...you'd think the man gets enough of me at home."

Molly laughs as we pass through the kitchen doors; I've no doubt her mind went straight into the gutter at my comment. "The man is smitten with you; it's written all over his face every time he lays eyes on ya."

I'm glad she can't see my face. I can't prevent the wince at her words, reminding me about the declaration Tobias made on Saturday. He hasn't said it again; as he acknowledged, he knows I'm not sure how I feel and his efforts of trying not to freak me out too much are appreciated.

Instead, I glance over my shoulder and roll my eyes at her, teasing, "You're such a romantic. Keep it up and I'll fire you."

Her eyes widen. "Watch—"

I walk straight into a brick wall.

Well, okay, not really. It just feels like one.

My upper arms are grabbed as I whip my head around to discover a giant standing in front of me.

Nope. Molly wasn't embellishing at all.

He's tall — taller than Tobias by about four inches — which puts him at about six and a half feet. And built. Really built. As in, there's no question he could snap me in two if he desired it, and I stiffen instantly in his grasp at the thought.

As my eyes reach his face, a stunned gasp escapes as I stare at him.

Curly black hair frames a breathtakingly handsome face; one that has eyes strikingly similar to my own gazing back at me.

"Who—What—" I take a deep breath as his lips curve in amusement at my obvious bewilderment. "Let go of me. I'm perfectly capable of standing on my own!"

"I'm sure you are." His voice is deep and accented, 'you are' said as 'yar,' as he does as requested. "Steady, yeah?"

A chuckle has me ripping my eyes from the strange man at the same time I realize Tobias has been standing beside him all along.

"Well, look at that." I cross my arms over my chest. "You're no longer the biggest man in the room, *husband*. Who's the giant?"

He steps forward, leaning in to give me a swift kiss on the lips, placing a hand on my lower back. "Let's go into your office."

"Molly—"

"Yep!"

Glad I don't even need to finish my request for her to take care of things up front, I turn and head back the way I came. Once we're inside, I sit behind the desk, awaiting an answer to my question.

"Joce, meet Ivor." Tobias pronounces it 'ee-vawr' and takes a seat across from me. "He's your bodyguard."

I suppose I should've seen that coming.

I purse my lips before shaking my head. "I don't think so."

"It's not up to you." He frowns at me. "He will follow

you everywhere. Most of the time, you won't even know he's there. It's a safety precaution."

"But—"

He shakes his head, cutting off my objection. "No. I told you I would protect you, but I can't be around all the time. Ivor will take excellent care of you. And if you don't tell me where you're at, he will. So, don't forget."

"Is he my bodyguard," I return with a scowl of my own. "Or my babysitter?"

Completely ignoring my attitude, he stands up and walks around the desk, pulling me into a hug. "Play nice. I have to get back. I'll see you after work."

"Oh! That reminds me." Deciding we'll discuss this later in private, I smile up at him. "I'm going to see Iris and Dexter for a little while after I'm done here."

He inclines his head, lowering his lips to mine for a brief kiss before saying softly, "Text me when you're on your way home then. And don't forget to take Ivor with you."

"Umm..." I cast a glance at Ivor. "Will you excuse us for a moment, please?"

The man nods and exits without a word.

"Does he know why?" I focus on Tobias once more. "And do I know him? I mean..." I lick my lips and his eyes narrow as he tugs me closer. "Did I know him? He looks familiar."

"You could say that. In case his hair and eyes didn't give it away, he was your brother. And yes, he's aware."

My jaw drops. "Really? But he's so huge compared to me!"

"All the better to protect you, my dear!" He winks at me before diverting my attention with his mouth and hands.

After a few moments, he leaves me wishing we were at home as he says goodbye, and my new shadow comes back into the room, ready to begin his duties.

"Please." I wave a hand at the chair across from mine. "Take a seat so we can chat for a few moments."

The moment Ivor sits he leans forward, hands folded on the edge of my desk as he grins at me. "You look well."

My head jerks back a bit at his words. "What?"

"Jórunnr." He stares at me, his eyes speculative as mine widen at the name I heard in one of my dreams. "Yeah, that's it. Last I saw you, you stole my knife and sliced your own throat." Dropping his gaze, he scrutinizes my neck — no doubt looking for the mark we both know is there — and nods. "Like I said, you're looking well."

Then he stands up and exits the room without another word.

Leaving me to wonder how I'm going to explain his presence to my friends later.

With a sigh, I push those thoughts aside and get back to work.

I KNOCK ON THE DOOR TO MY OLD APARTMENT, feeling awkward.

Ivor has agreed to stay outside and out of sight after I informed him that his presence will be difficult to explain to my friends, who are not aware of my apparent prior lives.

For some reason, he laughed when I said this but didn't say anything else.

I know eventually I'll have to come up with a reason as to why he's always around, but for now, I'm safe.

After all, I have a more pressing issue on my mind they need to focus on today.

Iris opens the door and rolls her eyes at me. "We let you keep the key so you could just let yourself in."

"I know." I smile self-consciously while stepping inside. "I feel weird about it, though. This isn't my place anymore."

She scoffs. "You know my home will always be your home. So knock it off and gimme a hug."

Throwing her arms around me without waiting for a response, I laugh. Moments later Dexter walks around the corner, joining in on the hug.

"Okay..." I breathe out as they squish me between them. "I have something I need to talk to you two about."

With that statement, they let go and shuffle me off to the living room.

Once we're sitting down — I'm in the middle of them — I glance at Dexter, then at Iris, before looking down at my hands.

"Don't freak out, but..." I take a deep breath, letting it out slowly as I ask, "what does love feel like? You know... the romantic relationship kind?"

I wince as Iris squeals, "What? Oh my gosh!"

Dexter doesn't say anything, yet I catch him smiling after sneaking a peek at his expression.

I hold up a hand as Iris goes to embrace me again. "It's not like that. I'm not sure what it's like, that's all. I want to know."

"Oh!" Iris claps her hands in excitement. "Love is amazing. The best thing in the world."

"The best? Even better than sex without love?" When she nods her head, face lighting up with what I'm sure are thoughts of her relationship with her boyfriend, I scoff in disbelief. "Sorry, I don't believe that's possible."

Dexter busts out laughing. "I'm not sure we can explain it to you, Jocelyn, especially when you've never felt it."

"Well, what's love to you?" I turn my face to focus on him. "What does it feel like?"

He lifts a brow. "You sure you wanna know?" I nod, and

he shrugs. "I'm a guy, so I don't know how it feels to a girl, but for me...it's wanting a specific girl like no other. I'm fascinated by her in every way; by her personality, her intelligence, her body. How alluring she is, and how much I want to figure out what makes her seem so mysterious even though she's open. And if she makes me happy — when the mere thought of her brings a smile to my face — I know I'm in trouble."

I tilt my head to the side, studying him for a moment, examining his words even as I acknowledge nobody has ever made me feel the way he's described.

I turn back to Iris. "How about you?"

Her eyes grow dreamy. "You know about when I met Garret. I was giddy and wanted to spend all my free time with him. I found him funny, smart, kind, and well, he's hot. I wanted to kiss him, and hug him, and fuck his brains out, all in one."

She grins as both Dexter and I laugh. "I just wanted to be around him, talk to him, see him...*all the time*. Even now, we've been together two years, and I feel the same. I adore him! It's like...lust and affection and devotion, all in one. I'd do anything for him, and he'd do anything for me."

"Yeah..." I bite my lip as I think of the right words to use, releasing it to ask, "but how do you *know* you're in love?"

The way they both look at me makes me feel as if I'm strange. I know it's not a question most people ask, but for some reason, I'm not sure how to decipher what such a feeling would, well, feel like.

It's Iris who questions me. "How do you feel about Tobias?"

"I dunno." I shrug when she glares at me. "I don't. I guess I never think about it."

"Well, think about it right now. How does he make you feel?"

I say the first thing that pops into my mind. "Frustrated."

Dexter busts out laughing while Iris rolls her eyes at me.

"Seriously," she remarks, frowning. "Examine your feelings. Do you hate him?"

"No."

"Do you like like him?"

"Huh? 'Like like' him? What kind of question is that?"

"There is like, for friendship." She points at herself, then at Dexter, before smiling at me. "You care about us, right?"

"Of course! I love you guys."

"Exactly. You care about us; you're attached to us. You don't want to murder us."

"I might if you don't get on with it."

With a giggle, she reaches out and takes my hand in hers. "Look. Do you like him more than a friend? Do you respect him, find him interesting, and think he's someone you want around for a long time?"

"Respect him? I suppose so. He's a hard worker, takes care of his family, has always been straight forward, and—"

"Okay, okay," she interrupts with a grimace. "Not what I meant. How about when you first had sex with him, you came home and basically told both of us that Luna was no longer. Was it him?"

Right. I take a deep breath because I'd never told them why I wasn't going out as Luna any longer; I simply said I became bored with the whole charade.

Looks like the time for the truth is here, no matter how much I don't want to say it out loud.

"Yes. We had sex and the way he knew exactly what I wanted...I..." When I pause, her nod gives me the encouragement to blurt out, "I was scared. He scared me. The way the sex blew my mind made me panic and then run away."

"So you felt a connection?"

Oh, if they only knew.

But I already told them about the dreams and, friends or not, I don't want to end up in a psych ward because they decide I've lost my mind. So I admit what I can. "Yeah, I guess you could call it that."

"Yay!" She grins, practically bouncing up and down in her seat. "This is—I'm so happy for you!"

"Me, too." Dexter speaks softly. "He's a good guy, and he seems to really like you."

I put on a happy face for both of them in response to that. Again, if they only had any idea of how he really felt; about how deep our connection went.

How much his declaration has me flustered.

"Also, I'm glad you look better." Dexter gives me a once over. "You worried us the other day."

"Thanks, I am fine." Well, it's partially true. "So, how are you guys doing? Enjoy having more room to yourselves?"

The topic changes easily and while they chatter away, reassuring me that they'd take me over free space any day, I'm left to think about what they said.

And wonder if I'll ever feel for Tobias the way my friends described.

What scares me is that I don't know the answer to the question...and more than anything else right now, I wish I did.

CHAPTER TWENTY-FIVE

One long work week involving repairs and upgrades — along with an early bedtime on Friday night thanks to exhaustion — leads to a rude awakening on Saturday.

The blankets are pulled off me, Tobias demanding, "Get up, sleepyhead! I've got plans for you."

"Do they involve breakfast in bed with a side of sex?" I mumble, using my pillow to block out the bright light. "Because if not...go away."

"Nah." He pauses, then, "You're not really a morning person are you?"

Gee, he's just figuring that out?

"Too early." *Leave me to sleep*, I wail in my head. "I'm tired."

"It's eleven in the morning!"

His voice is tinged with amusement, but I'm just

feeling grumpy.

"Any time before I want to get up is too early." I clutch the pillow tighter to block out as much noise as possible as well. "Shoo."

"Okay." He sighs in an exaggerated fashion. "You asked for it."

With a firm grip, he grabs my bare feet by the ankles. My body tightens, the response instantaneous thanks to my intense fear of being tickled, something I hate more than being woken up before I'm ready.

"Shh." He chuckles, sliding his hands up my calves, shocking the hell out of me as he begins massaging them simultaneously. "Relax."

As he squeezes the muscles, a moan escapes before I can think of doing otherwise, and my aching body gives way to his caring touch. Even though I sit more than my other employees get to during their shirts, standing most of my day is the usual way of things. I'm involved in everything, and twelve hours on your feet is a killer.

"Aren't you glad you hired Nicole? I don't even want to imagine how grumpy you were before you had another manager to assist."

"You mean before I had a man that wouldn't let me sleep? I was just fine, thank you."

"I'm sorry." He raises his voice a bit, laughing. "I can't hear you from under that pillow."

"Maybe you should clear your ears."

"What?"

"I said—"

"Huh? Oh wait, I can hear you fine." He slaps my ass out of nowhere, making me yelp in surprise. "Your naked body is distracting, though."

Lifting the pillow off and away from my head, I shove it to the side. When I try to roll over, though, he has other ideas.

"Oh no, you don't." Putting his hand into the middle of my back, he holds me down. "There has been a slight change of plans."

I bet there has been, but I wouldn't be me if I didn't mess with him a bit.

"Do they involve me going back to sleep?" I yawn as if bored. "If not, I'm not interested."

He smacks my ass again.

"Hey!" I rise up on my elbows and glare at him over my shoulder. "What's that for?"

"New rule," he responds with a grin. "Anything I want to do is interesting."

When I bust out laughing, he climbs onto the bed and slides up until his body covers mine, hands on each side of my head. His breath against my neck makes me want him closer, the simple knowledge of what's coming turning me on.

"You're so warm." I lift my ass up, rubbing against his perfectly placed and ready for me cock, teasing, "Too bad I don't have sex with men who rudely awaken me by stealing the blankets and leaving me out in the cold."

"Aw." His response and tone are a mix of mocking and amusement. "Are you cold? Here. Let me warm you up."

One hand leaves my line of vision as he holds himself up with the other. He grabs a pillow and tugs it out of sight, before returning with the hand and skimming it down my side. He grabs my hip.

"Lift up."

Wanting — no, *needing* — his cock in me this instant, I do as he demands, lowering my forehead to the bed simultaneously. After sliding the pillow beneath my hips, he curves his body around mine as he guides himself to my entrance. Slipping the tip up and down the outside, he kisses the back of my neck and shoulders as I moan at his teasing.

"Do you want me to warm you up, babe?" He enters me, just the tip, before pulling back out, and I push back in response. "Beg me."

I wiggle, enjoying the sharp intake of breath he takes, and tell him, "Fuck me, now."

"That doesn't sound like you begging."

Smiling even though he can't see me, I stretch my arms out, which naturally arches my back as I squirm against him as much as possible. "I want you to please fuck me now."

"You are, without a doubt, the most stubborn woman

I've ever met," he informs me, "and I love you for it. I wouldn't have you any other way than how you are: beautiful, intelligent and insanely obstinate."

Before I can reply to him saying that, he enters me with one swift thrust. I gasp, clutching the sheets to anchor myself, his now free hand wrapping itself in my hair. He slowly pulls my head back, murmuring, "And mine. Can't forget you belong to me."

I whimper as he withdraws to the tip, crying out when he plunges back in once more.

"Do you belong to me Joce?" He pauses when our bodies are barely touching again, his grip on my hair firm as he tugs to keep my attention. "Tell me, love. Say it."

It's a weird moment to feel like crying, but I do.

I feel lost, even as I've never felt more present in my life.

Never felt more wanted or more desired.

His words call to a part of me I'm not sure I want to listen to right now. A place that tells me I *do* belong to him when I've never felt as if I ever belonged to anyone, anywhere. Not even as a child, not even knowing how much my parents loved me — parents that I know now took in a little girl that nobody knew where she came from and treated her as their own.

Our connection is undeniable; our bodies made for each other.

And I love it and hate it all in one.

Because I can't fight it and I'm not sure I should.

So, as a tear he can't see rolls down my cheek and is absorbed into the sheets, I whisper, "I'm yours. All yours."

"And I'm yours, love." He releases my hair, and I lower my head back to the bed as he grabs my hips with both hands. "All our lives, no matter when or where. And I'm all the more ecstatic I finally got to make you mine in every single fucking way possible."

He buries himself to the hilt on the last word, my hips grasped tightly as he pulls back out and back in, over and over. Each stroke is ferocious; savage in its intensity, each stroke symbolic of the power we hold over each other. Him, unable to resist me, and I, unable to refuse him, our bodies moving together perfectly.

A hand snakes around to the front, toying with my clit, the pace of his thrusts in harmony with the massage of his fingers. It's all I can do to focus on the sweet pleasure of his hands on me, my orgasm building, his words flowing over me.

"The first night, it was all I could do to keep my hands off you long enough to eat." All the way in, he pauses with a groan, pulling me tight against him and holding me there. "I told myself I should wait to have you as yourself, not disguised as Luna; when you knew who I was and how much you meant to me. However, I knew you wouldn't let me in any other way."

He picks up the pace again, each thrust making it

impossible for me to speak as my orgasm closes in. "The sex was fucking fantastic, and when you bolted, I knew I would do anything to get you into my bed permanently."

He pulls out and flips me over, tossing the pillow aside as he places my feet on his shoulders. Holding me still with a grip on my legs, he sheaths his cock in my pussy once more, so fast and hard I can barely catch a breath.

"Oh god...Tobias...I'm... please..."

I know I'm incoherent, but every thrust, every plunge is at a pace that seems impossible and leaves me panting, wanting this moment to never end.

I close my eyes as his fingers find my clit, his thumb stroking around and around until I'm frantic. My body instinctively tightens up as the impending orgasm hovers on the edge, just out of my reach.

"Please..."

I don't know what I'm begging for, my fists clenching in the sheets as I open my eyes and catch Tobias' gaze.

"I..." Swallowing, I lift my chin a little. "Please."

He removes his fingers from my clit, using it to hold himself up as he leans forward, my legs still straight, and wraps his hand around my throat.

Just enough to restrict my breathing.

Enough for a sob to escape as he gazes at me, his desire blazing in his eyes as he thrusts, our bodies rubbing perfectly to send the pleasure soaring even higher. "Come with me, Joce. You ready?"

I don't even get to answer as my climax spreads through me, the hand around my throat tightening as he strokes deep one last time and pauses, covering my mouth with his own as he moans into it. He pulls out and back in, hand continuing to grasp my neck as his tongue seeks entrance to my mouth, and I let him in.

My legs fall to wrap around his waist, and his hand leaves my throat. I wrap my arms around his neck as he cradles the back of mine, his kisses continuing to steal my breath as we lie connected, close as two people can be.

After a few moments, he pulls back and grins down at me. "Time for your surprise."

I nod, because, at this moment, I'm pretty sure I'll follow this man anywhere.

A thought that doesn't alarm me like it would have only a few weeks ago, and has me smiling up at him, ready for anything he can throw at me.

❦

"You're taking me skating?"

As we get out of the car, he laughs. "Please tell me you know how to skate."

"Are you kidding me? Of course, I do." Shutting my door, I walk over to him. "I'll skate circles around you."

I'm exaggerating a little. I haven't been skating since I turned twelve.

"Ha. You can try. I'm a pro."

I roll my eyes at him. "Sure you are." Glancing around the parking lot, I comment, "It sure looks busy here today. Then again, it is Saturday."

"Yep." He puts his arm around me and squeezes. "Don't worry, I won't let you out of my sight."

Within moments, we're inside. After he pays for us and we get a ticket for skates, we head through the next set of doors.

As we turn right, my mouth drops open as everyone — my friends and his family — yell "Surprise!"

Confused, I stare at their smiling faces.

Tobias leans down and speaks into my ear. "Happy Birthday, Joce."

I glance up at him, then back at them, before returning to his once more. "Um..."

He frowns. "What's wrong?"

There's no way to express what I feel to him in that moment.

Confused. Angry. Lost.

I take a step back. He attempts to tighten his hold, but I smack his hand away, turning around and running right back out the doors as tears blur my vision. I lean against the building as the memory of my last conversation with my father takes over.

"You lied to me!" I glare at him, pissed that he hid

something like this from me all my life. "Why wouldn't you tell me?"

His eyes begged me to understand. "You were just a little girl. You clung to your mother and I as if we were your lifelines. We weren't sure if you remembered or not, but you were so happy. You adjusted with no issues, started school, made friends; we didn't want to bring it up because you were ours in every way that counted."

I stare down at the birth certificate in my hands, bile rising in my throat. "Is any of this true? My name? My birthdate?"

He shakes his head. "No. You told us your name was Jocelyn, so we kept that, but the rest, we gave to you. Your birthdate is the day we met you, and you put your tiny little hands in ours. You needed a birthday."

"How old am I?"

"You told everyone you were three; we had no reason to think differently. As far as I know, you're eighteen. That's all that matters."

In that moment, I hate him. Hate him for keeping this from me, hate him and my mother for not thinking about how it would make me feel to know my whole life is made up because nobody could verify my identity, and hate him for thinking that what they thought was all that mattered. For him still thinking that's all that matters.

"It's not all that matters," I scream. "I'm a made-up name, with a made up birthday! I hate you for saying that."

"Luna. Honey..."

He tries to pull me into his arms, but I slam my fists against his shoulders. "No! Don't touch me! I hate you."

Whirling around, I leave before he can say anything else.

Before I say anything else I might regret.

Tobias' familiar scent surrounds me as he crouches down beside me, wrapping me in his arms.

As sobs rack my body, I hate myself at this moment; for ruining his surprise, for continuing to be hurt and angry over something my father couldn't help.

And for wishing I had the answers I'm never going to get.

"I—I'm sorry," I choke out when I can finally speak.

"Shh." He strokes a hand down my hair, kissing the top of my head. "I'm not angry, just worried. Tell me what I did wrong."

Shaking my head, I lift my eyes to look into his. "N-nothing. I...I don't celebrate my birthday b-because it's not real."

It takes him a moment, but I see the realization dawn in his gaze, in his face. He grits his teeth, lifting a hand to wipe away the tear sliding down my cheek, whispering, "Now *I'm* the sorry one."

I can't even smile, my lower lip quivering. "Did I ruin the party?"

"Nah. They just wanna know you're okay." He stands

up slowly, taking me with him. Once we're both on my feet, he takes my hand in his. "I can send them a message telling them to hide all the stuff and get rid of the presents."

He pulls out his phone, and I cover it with my free hand. "No, don't do that. We'll tell them they shocked me is all."

"Are you sure? They'll understand if I explain."

I nod, taking a deep breath and letting it out slowly. "I don't want to ruin their fun. Although, I'm surprised Iris and Dexter didn't tell you I don't celebrate it."

He laughs as we walk back toward the doors. "Oh, they did. It was my fault I didn't listen."

"You? Not listen? I'm shocked."

He smacks my ass, then pulls me against him, kissing my temple. "Take two?"

"Yep."

We re-enter, hand in hand.

I see the curiosity on everyone's faces and smile brightly. "Sorry all, you shocked the shit out of me!"

They all laugh and greet me with hugs.

When Tobias drags me over to get skates, I have a feeling the fun is just beginning.

CHAPTER TWENTY-SIX

After we're all laced up, Tobias leads us both to the floor, hand in hand.

Even though it's been over a decade since I last skated, it's not long before I rediscover my rhythm. At first, Tobias is content to skate next to me, holding my hand, but I see the exact moment the part that wants to compete takes over.

He releases his hold, moving in front of me, and turns to face me as he skates backward. "Ready to skate circles around me, love?"

"Nah."

"Come on." He looks over his shoulder to make sure no one is behind him, then returns his mischievous gaze to me. "What about a race?"

I glance around, noticing every single other person

here leaving the rink, and shrug. "Sure, why not? It seems like you planned it anyway."

"Sure did." Stopping as we round the corner, he lines up with the entrance to one side of the rink, and points to the ground. "We start right here. First person to return back here wins."

With a nod, I smile sweetly and ask, "What's the prize?"

"No prize." He grins. "Just for the win."

"Who is judging?"

Everyone has lined up around the wall, and he points to the right of the starting line, where his mother stands next to Dexter.

"They are. One for both of us, so it's fair." He winks and positions himself. "Ready?"

"Now, now Toby. You know that's my line!" His mother says with a laugh. "On three."

"Yeah, Toby," I jibe, ruining it with a snicker. "You picked the wrong person to race."

"And you, love, underestimate how fast I am. I did run cross-country in high school, y'know."

No, I didn't, but he seems to be missing one important fact. "You know we're skate-racing, not running, correct?"

"One!"

"Both require speed, don't they?" He tosses me another wink. "See you at the end."

"Two!"

"Yep, see you there, *munchkin*." I blow him a kiss, both of us laughing as we face forward.

"Three!"

We both take off like a shot, and he immediately starts outpacing me.

I admit, I'm impressed. No matter how fast I skate, I won't catch up to him.

And I almost let him have his honest win. Almost.

That is until he turns around and starts to skate backward, waving at me with a triumphant grin on his face.

I make as if I'm about to fall, twirling my arms before tucking and rolling while still trying to make the fall look as natural as possible — and, of course, me attempting to save myself from being hurt. I swear I hear everyone on the outside of the rink gasp and suck in their breaths.

And like a fool, he takes the bait.

Before I know it, he's crouched beside me as I get back on all the wheels, my hands against the ground to hold steady. I focus my gaze on the ground as he touches my shoulder.

"Joce, are you all right?"

Peeking at him from the corner of my eye, I make certain that when I push him, he'll land on his ass. Lifting my eyes, I meet his and smile. "Gotcha."

Bumping him, his ass meets the floor, hands too busy

trying to catch himself to grab me as I scramble away, and take off.

Hoots of laughter rise up from everyone as I skate fast as possible, not daring to look behind me while crossing over the finish line. Dexter and Iris rush over, laughing as they hug me.

"Remind me," Tobias comments as he approaches, "to add cunning to the list of qualities I love about you."

"Hey, you're the one that fell for it." I can't keep the grin from my face as Iris and Dexter release me. "No pun intended."

I squeal, Tobias pulling me against him before I know what's happening, lowering his lips to mine. He keeps the kiss short and sweet, but that doesn't keep Iris from clapping giddily, as Randolf yells, "Get a room!"

We pull apart with a laugh, Tobias taking my hand in his, as his mother waves at us from the sidelines.

"Cake time!"

"Oh, you can't be serious." I glare at Tobias. "You went so far as to get me a cake?"

"Technically, my mother made it."

"I'm so paying you back for this later." We approach the table where everyone is standing around chatting. "Just so you know."

"How about we call it even," he whispers in my ear. "That way, I don't get you back later for your little trick."

I slide into the seat he indicates, not responding to his words, and look up as he lights the candles.

Iris and Dexter sit next to me, while the rest fill in the extra seats or stand around the table.

Tobias starts off the singing, holding my gaze with his own, but as they all join in, tears fill my eyes.

Only this time, they are happy tears.

Because I finally recognize one thing.

I'm surrounded by people who want me around: either by marriage or by friendship.

And, whether or not it's truly my birthday, they don't care.

They simply love me.

Just like my parents who raised me as their own.

By the time they reach the end of the song my enjoyment is genuine and for the first time in my adult life, I blow out the candles on my cake, making a wish that everything stays like it is.

Which ends up being a foolish thing to do.

Because, of course, a discovery brought to my attention not long after the party means my life will never be the same again.

A WEEK AFTER OUR DAY AT THE SKATING RINK, MR.

Cain shows up at our house in the late evening, unannounced.

Having finished dinner not long before, Tobias and I sit on the couch watching TV when the doorbell rings. I pause the show as he gets up to answer the door, only to return moments later requesting I join him and the lawyer in the study.

Sitting down in the chair next to Tobias, Mr. Cain takes the seat behind the desk.

"What's this about, Brandon?" Tobias seems annoyed as I look over at him, mouth set in a grim line. "It's quite late for you to show up here without calling first."

"Again, I apologize." His words are rushed as if he can't get them out fast enough. "I came because I received a request from another client of mine and I don't believe it should wait."

"What does any client of yours, besides me, have to do with my wife?"

I was looking at Tobias, but now I swing my head until my eyes land on Mr. Cain. "Me?"

Mr. Cain locks his gaze on mine with a nod. "A client of mine saw your wedding photo in the paper. She sent me here to ask you a couple questions because she believes you may be related."

Family.

I grip the arms of the chair, my heart picking up pace as it pounds, my palms growing slick with my sudden anxiety. My eyes never leave Mr. Cain's, who is watching me with a frown, and I feel Tobias pry my hand from its death grip on the chair and interlace our fingers.

"W-what are the questions?" I can barely breathe through the sudden tightening inside my chest, but I must know. "How does she believe we're related?"

"First, I'd like to show you a picture." He stands up and walks around the desk, perching on the end and extends his hand. "Go on, take it."

I reach out and take it.

I don't know what I expect when I see it, but I know it wasn't to feel as if I've been punched in the gut.

Because peering up at me from the photo is a woman who could be my twin, except she's probably in her mid-to-late thirties; in her arms, an infant, while an older teen with the same black hair stands beside her, glaring angrily at the camera.

Tears prick my eyes. Tobias is downright motionless next to me, but I'm riveted by this picture, unable to look at him as I ask, "Who is she?"

"Mrs—Jocelyn," Mr. Cain says softly, "I need to know...do you have any marks that would qualify as identifying? Such as a birthmark?"

The lady in the picture smiles up at me, but I finally drag my eyes away to meet Mr. Cain's. "Yes, I have a few."

He picks up another photo from the pile in his hand and holds it out to me.

This time, it's a picture of a baby, and I gasp, nearly dropping the photo when my eyes zero in on the distinctive mark on the child's chest.

The same mark I examined in the mirror on the morning of my wedding, although it was lighter now and less noticeable than the one in the picture.

A sob escapes, and Tobias squeezes my hand, saying, "Get to the point Brandon before you upset my wife any further. Who does your client believe Jocelyn is to her?"

"The woman — the one holding the infant in the photograph — believes you may be her grandchild. The girl standing next to her was her daughter, your mother, who had just turned seventeen a week before your birth."

I glare up at him, holding the photos out to him. "Why now? I'm adopted after I was found by strangers on a street."

Okay, I don't know if that's actually what happened, but I'm angry at this moment and not sure what the hell is going on; wondering why this woman would suddenly be interested enough to contact me through her lawyer.

His eyes fill with pity, shaking his head. "I'm sorry, but they didn't give you away."

Now I'm just confused, my voice rising at his unspoken implications. "What do you mean? As far as I know, my parents adopted me when I was three. Are you calling them liars?"

"Brandon, what the—"

Mr. Cain holds up a hand, staying the beginning of Tobias' angry tirade, and holds out a piece of paper this time. When I take it, I realize it's a birth certificate.

"Juliette Lorraine West," I read out loud. "Date of birth: August tenth, nineteen ninety-one. Mother: Amanda Francis West—"

"No fucking way!"

My head jerks up at Tobias' outburst, but Mr. Cain jumps in before he can speak. "We'll need to do a DNA test, but I'm fairly sure—"

"Get out!" Tobias points to the door. "Right now!"

"Hey!" I rise out of my chair, standing in between the two while facing Tobias. "I want to hear what he has to say."

His eyes blaze. "You don't understand—"

"And I won't," I interrupt him, "if you don't let me hear what he has to say!"

Whirling to face Mr. Cain, I hold everything he handed me up in his face. "Well, Mr. Cain? None of this proves anything. I was adopted at age three. So, what does this woman want with me? Obviously, I was given away by her daughter—"

Again, he shakes his head. "I'm sorry, but her grandchild wasn't given away. That picture of the girl in her grandmother's arms? She was a week old."

"And?"

He takes a deep breath, suddenly looking tired as he

says, "The following morning after that picture was taken, her daughter, the child, and the nanny went missing. Two days later, the child and nanny were still nowhere to be found, the child's mother found dead in a nearby alley."

And just like that, my world spins around me, my hand dropping to my side, the items in my hand float to the floor as he finishes with, "Amanda was an only child, her child the only grandchild of the West family, and the sole heiress to a fortune."

The last thing I recall is Tobias calling Mr. Cain a son of a bitch and telling him to get the fuck out.

CHAPTER TWENTY-SEVEN

THERE'S SOMETHING ABOUT GETTING THE ANSWERS I've always wanted that makes me realize, perhaps I really don't want them all.

What's the saying?

Ah, yes.

Too little, too late.

I'm lying in bed early the next morning, curled into a ball on my side as Tobias sleeps next to me.

I woke up, and unable to fall back asleep, I logged onto the computer to read up on the West family. Something I wish I hadn't done.

Too little, too late, indeed.

It didn't take long before I turned the computer back off and crawled back into bed.

Which brings me back to lying here in bed, listening to

him snore beside me. I wish I could forget what I've been told and what I read this morning.

And there is no doubt in my mind I'm the missing child even without a test to verify the DNA.

I'm not sure whether to laugh or cry.

Laugh because Tobias' comments about me always being the rich one were true and I'm simply astounded at finding out I'm most likely in line to become one of the richest heiresses in the world.

A terrifying thought for a girl who has always had 'just enough.'

As for crying, I'm definitely closer to sobbing than laughing.

According to every single article I could find, of which there were many, Amanda West had been found murdered in an alley, her daughter and the nanny nowhere to be found, exactly as Mr. Cain had told us. There were pictures, but I hadn't looked. I didn't want to know.

Following a search and pleas from the family — mainly her mother and father, Marshall and Francis West — for the nanny to bring the child home, or for anyone with information to step forward, nothing ever happened. It seemed as if the nanny and child had disappeared into thin air.

But then the article listed the nanny's name and picture. I didn't remember the name, but I knew her face.

It wasn't even a memory, but a recognition I couldn't ignore.

She'd been my *mommy*, the woman I searched for so frantically in my dream before stepping outside.

And all I want to know is 'why?'

Why would she steal me? What purpose did it serve? Did she just want a child and so she took the first one she could get her hands on?

And how had she done it? Had killing my mother been a part of the plan or had she been running away?

It couldn't have been about the money. There had never been any ransom demands, at least none were mentioned in any of the new articles.

A tear slips out, making it clear I have to stop thinking about this, but I can't.

Because even worse than knowing someone stole me from my family, is the knowledge this discovery will take me away from the one I've just acquired.

I'm honest enough to admit to myself that I want to meet this woman who thinks I'm her granddaughter. Not because she's rich, but because she may be family.

Family. Something I never thought I'd have again after my parents died, leaving me without any relatives.

There's no way to ignore the fact I may have a connection with someone other than by choice and by marriage.

As another tear slips down my cheek, Tobias wraps his

arms around me from behind, pressing a soft kiss against my shoulder. He doesn't say anything, but I feel the need to explain why I'm sniffling at five a.m. instead of sleeping.

"It's weird." I cough to clear my throat and wipe at my eyes. "How it feels like everything that has happened so far was for a reason. I hate that saying, but if I hadn't married you, my picture most likely wouldn't have been in a newspaper, and this woman wouldn't have found me."

"You don't know she's right." His words join another kiss on my shoulder before his mouth moves up toward the nape of my neck. "But if you want to know for sure, we will find out, love. I hate it when you cry, especially when your happiness is the most important thing to me."

The sweetness of his words, the kindness of his voice, don't soothe me; instead, my silent tears escalate into full-on sobs. He gently turns me around, tucking my head against his chest, and strokes my hair for a little while.

Eventually, he reaches away for a second, coming back with a tissue, which I promptly use. Then, after excusing myself to the bathroom, I return to the bed and back into his arms, cuddling against him.

After a few moments, he kisses the top of my head, sighing. "My first thought when Brandon told you, other than how much of an asshole he was to tell you like he did, was 'story of my life' and how much it figures that this time around, I'd marry you and get you into my bed, only to have something like this happen."

VIOLET HAZE

"I know how you feel about me," I reply softly. "And we do have an agreement, but if I am this child...I can't ignore it. I need to..."

He tightens his hold on me as my voice fades away. "Joce, in this regard, our agreement and what I want comes second."

"And my diner..."

"Yes." He tilts my chin up, holding it in place as he gives me a brief kiss on the lips. "It's all yours now, no matter what happens."

"But—"

"Shh." Putting a finger against my mouth to silence me, he rolls me under him as he continues, "I love you. I wanted you, so I did whatever it took to get you in my life, in my bed. If what he said is true, I know you; you'll want to go there, meet your family. I get it. I understand completely. But it was never about that diner. It's one hundred percent yours. Got it?"

It's pitch black, yet as I nod, I know he's smiling at me. The subtle change in his intentions is clear as his cock hardens against my belly.

His hand — the one with a finger resting against my lips to silence me — moves, sliding down to cup the back of my neck as his mouth descends on mine, seeking immediate entrance with a teasing caress of his tongue. Granting him access, I bring my arms up and wrap them around his neck, sliding my hands up into his hair while he deepens our kiss.

Our tongues engaged in a leisurely battle, he adjusts his body until he's lying on his side next to me, skimming his free hand down to my breast. Cupping it, my nipple instantly tightens, seeking his attention with an almost desperation he doesn't ignore.

Flicking his thumb back and forth over it, he chuckles into my mouth, catching my tongue between his teeth for a brief nip before releasing it. He moves to the other breast, repeating the action until I'm arching into his hand, wanting and needing more.

Instead of obliging, he presses me back to the bed and glides his hand down, and down. Stopping right before where his hand is most wanted, he drags his mouth away as he commands, "Spread your legs."

I don't argue. I'm not in the mood to play games. I want to have his touch on me everywhere and forget, for just a little while, that everything is about to change. I do as he says, only for him to say, "More."

Then he taps me between the legs, enough to get my attention, yet not hurt me.

"Ooh!" I gasp, opening my legs a bit more while laughing in complete surprise. "There. How's that?"

"Perfect."

When he taps me again, harder this time, my eyes flutter closed as I moan, my arousal heightened. As he does it once more, it smarts, yet the sting is so sweet, an unbidden sob of need escaping. He keeps his hand there where it lands, using two fingers to slip inside my pussy, his thrusting sending trembles of delight through me.

"I knew you'd like that." The words are thick with desire, pulling his fingers out and teasing my clit by circling it. "You're so wet."

I can't even respond, whimpering as his two fingers thrust back inside, his thumb continuing to torment my clit, relief nowhere in sight. His fingers curl up inside me, caressing my g-spot, and I grab his hair tighter while I try to fuck his hand.

Between his movements and mine, my orgasm rapidly approaches. It's his voice that yanks me over the edge.

"God, you're gorgeous, love." He puts his mouth against mine and whispers, "Come for me."

Then he pulls his hand out and smacks just right, fusing our lips and catching my cry as I orgasm. While I tremble, he repositions himself over my body and wraps one of my legs around his waist, his cock fucking me within seconds.

"I can't go slow." I barely recognize what he says, jumbled as they are against my mouth. "Hard and fast is what I need."

I move my hands to his shoulders, wrapping my other leg around his waist, holding on for dear life as he grasps one hip and slams into me.

Each stroke in and out has me gasping, my nails digging in, as he possesses me with his body.

Showing me I'm what he wants, what he needs, what he loves.

And when it's over, his body coming down over mine, the weight is delicious.

I stroke his back before the urge to hug him and memorize this moment has me stopping abruptly.

Perhaps I feel way more than I'm willing to admit and I'm not sure exactly to do with the way I'm feeling because it's something I've never experienced before.

But, then he's kissing me, and once more, I'm pulled away from my thoughts by the one person who seems to know exactly when I need such a thing.

Especially since the future will come soon enough.

CHAPTER TWENTY-EIGHT

IF THERE IS ONE THING I'VE LEARNED SINCE MEETING Tobias, it is the truth about how money can absolutely buy anything.

Not that he has such an attitude. Matter of fact, his low-key way of living really appeals to me. He's got a nice car, a nice house, and he dresses for his position, but a show-off? Not at all.

When I asked him why he didn't have a driver or lots of staff, he told me it's because he doesn't need it. He's perfectly capable of driving himself around, and making himself food, etcetera. Sure, it would be easier to let people do these activities for him, but his money is better spent on other things.

Which apparently includes a faster turnaround for DNA.

Mr. Cain returned to the house Sunday, making sure

to apologize for the way he approached the subject of my parentage with both of us, something I instantly forgave him for. After all, the man had a job to do, and it *is* an unsolved mystery to this day. Who wouldn't be excited about potentially solving it?

Like I said, all was forgiven, and at Tobias' insistence, both samples were sent to a facility of his choosing.

And that's how, five days after the initial conversation with Mr. Cain, I'm sitting at my desk at work when Tobias comes in and hands me a letter.

A letter which informs me I am indeed related to Francis West.

Even though I knew we were related the moment I saw the picture — our resemblance is uncanny — I still gasp at seeing the words on paper.

I glance up, my eyes locking on Tobias, who is slouched in the chair and staring at me. His face unreadable, I stand up and walk over to him; he straightens so I may sit on his lap, which I do.

He wraps his arms around my waist but doesn't do or say anything.

I'm not even sure what to say at this moment, so I state the obvious. "We're related." I lick my lips and his eyes instantly focus on them. "Did you tell Mr. Cain?"

"No need." His gaze never leaves my mouth. "Your... grandmother contacted him to inform him, along with giving him permission to give you her contact information."

"Do you have it?"

Tobias reaches into his jacket, pulling out a piece of paper from the inside pocket, and holds it out. When I try to take it from his hand, he doesn't let go, saying, "She wants you to do more than simply call her. She is hoping you will go there."

"And I will—"

"Tomorrow," he cuts in. "She'd like you to show up tomorrow."

Surprised, I suck in a breath as he releases the paper into my grasp. "That's so soon."

"You can say no."

"I know that—" I stop, taking in the tortured look he's trying to hide, yet failing at. "Do you want me to say no?"

"Yes. No!" He frowns, removing one arm from around my waist to shove it through his hair in a show of frustration. "It's not like that. I know you want to get to know them, but tomorrow is too soon."

"Not for her," I point out. "To her, it's been twenty-eight years."

"You're awfully calm about this."

"Would me flipping out do any good?" I'm sure many people would think my reaction is rather abnormal, but it wouldn't do me any good to flip out, or cry, or make myself sick about it. "Is it going to change the facts? Besides, I've had five days to get used to the idea I may be someone else."

"Five days? That's all you need? Do you hear yourself?"

I throw my hands up, jumping off his lap, and scowl at him. "What do you want me to say? I'm not like most people; even you should know that by now! I refuse to flip out about something I *can't* change."

I toss the papers on my desk with a frustrated huff. "Nothing I do or say will make this any easier. Crying about it won't change the fact I was abducted. It won't change the fact my whole life is a *lie*. What good would doing anything but meeting this woman do for me?"

"Joce—"

"No." I hold up a hand because we both know I've already made a decision. "I'm going."

He pulls me back down into his lap, growling at me, as he positions my body so we face each other straight on. "Look at me."

Crossing my arms over my chest, I keep silent even while doing as he demands.

"First, I already told you I support you in this." He grasps my upper arms, then smiles. "Do I want you to go tomorrow? No, of course not. We've not even been married a month, and I've certainly not had enough of fucking you either. I'm certain I never will."

Damn him, but I can't resist my lips quirking up at his statement, and relax a little in his lap.

"You're living with me, and I'm still worried about your safety. I can't leave my work to come with you longer than it takes to get you there, which means I can't protect you. I may be the boss, but you know me, even now I'm very involved in my work. All I can do is send Ivor with you and hope it's enough."

With a slide of his hand to the back of my neck, he tugs me closer and kisses my lips softly. "I'm not in charge here. I don't own you; I can't make you stay. I'm dominant, and I love my control, but I'm not an asshole. I want to make you stay, lock you in my imaginary dungeon, and keep you safe from a threat we both know is out there. Yet, even if that were something I could do, you're cunning enough to find a way to get out anyhow."

I can't help my laughter because his assessment is undeniable.

"I respect you, love." The words are low, his voice fierce. "You're intelligent, tough, and brave. I don't know anyone else who would've handled the news the way you have; it makes me proud to call you mine. But, it doesn't mean I can't worry for you because this is unlike anything else you've experienced. You're walking into a whole different life. Even if you're Jocelyn to yourself, to me, to your friends, and to many others, you are Juliette to this woman. You are her lost grandchild, her legacy, and from what Brandon said, the future of the West family's empire."

"I know. I've thought about this a lot."

"Do you?" At my nod, he sighs, pulling my body flush against his and hugs me. "As long as you're aware of that. And the need to be careful. You've got people you can trust here, but you can't be sure there. Don't go anywhere without Ivor. Don't be alone with anyone. *That* is what I'm telling you to do. And if you need me, let me know. I may believe you need to meet this woman without any distractions, including me, but it doesn't mean I won't come there and kick some ass if it's needed."

All of a sudden, I feel sad, because he's saying so much more than his words convey.

"You're saying goodbye without really saying goodbye, aren't you?" I lift my head to scrutinize his face. "You don't think I'll come back, do you?"

His whole demeanor changes, his eyes darkening, the misery in them evident. "Not goodbye. Only you can end what's between us. But you'll be eight hours away, love. Your whole life is about to change forever, and even if you desire it, you won't get to keep both identities. You can't be Jocelyn the local diner owner who helps run her business, and Juliette, the West family heiress."

I open my mouth to object, but he shakes his head. "I know you won't believe that right now, but you'll see. You're no longer a 'made-up name, with a made-up birthdate,' to use your words. If this goes public, which I've no doubt it will, everything will change."

Hearing this makes me pause. I didn't lie when I said I've thought a lot about this. I have, and I know what it means. He's right, I am smart; enough to acknowledge he has a point.

I do worry about the distance. The eight hours distance is driving, but even flying, it may not be conducive to two lives — or to our marriage being able to survive. I'm not quite sure how I feel about that.

It's the idea of becoming a part of the public eye that scares me the most. It will put my face all over, making it all the easier for anyone who wants to hurt me to find me. I will never be a 'nobody' ever again.

"I understand. But even with all the things that could happen, I have to go. I need to."

"Then I will make arrangements and take you there myself."

I spend the rest of the evening setting up for things to get taken care of at the diner while I'm gone, then head to Iris and Dexter's after work to fill them in.

Both are incredulous when I inform them of my real identity, and fill them in on where I'm heading tomorrow.

"She found you from the picture?" Sitting on the couch, both of them look confused, but Iris is the one who asks the questions. "How did she know it was you?"

"She didn't. We had DNA tests to make sure."

"Wow." Iris stands up and hugs me. "I'm so excited for you. You'll have to let us know how it goes. What does Tobias think?"

"He's supportive." I return her embrace with a smile. "He knows this is important to me."

"Good. Do you know how long you'll be gone?"

"No, everything is one day at a time right now."

Dexter joins in on the hug as I tell them, "I'll miss you two!"

Sentiments they return as I promise to keep in touch, and shortly after, I leave to head home.

And just like that, the end of my life as I know it collides with a whole new one.

CHAPTER TWENTY-NINE

AFTER IVOR, TOBIAS, AND I GET INTO THE CAR SENT TO pick us up from the airport, my desire to throw up increases with every passing mile.

Yesterday, following my call to the number Mr. Cain had written on the piece of paper where nobody picking up, I dialed Mr. Cain himself.

"I'm unable to tell you anything personal," he informed me after I asked why she hadn't answered the phone. "Are you planning to show up tomorrow as she requested?"

"Yes."

"Excellent. Shall I give her a specific time you will be there?"

After telling him six p.m., he said he would pass the message on and wished me well, then hung up.

Now here I am, about to meet Francis — that is, my grandmother— for the first time. Also assuming I will meet my grandfather, Marshall, since I didn't find anything indicating he died, but I can't be sure.

Tobias has his arm around my shoulders, and at my sigh, he tugs me snug against his side. "You all right?"

"Yeah." A pause, then, "I suppose I'm a bit nervous."

"I imagine anyone would be." He chuckles and kisses the top of my head. "Just remember, you can call me anytime."

"I know."

"Good. Now, keep in mind that Ivor will be closer to you than at home. Make sure they give him a room near to you, shouting distance preferred."

"Right." At his name, Ivor drags his gaze away from the window to pay attention. "And how do I explain him being necessary exactly?"

Tobias grins. "You don't. Chances are they have no idea who you are, or of the danger you may be in, but you can never be too careful. This is why I said to be cautious about who you trust. Being we now know you are a missing heiress to one of the richest families in the country, they will think nothing of you having security."

"Oh, I see."

"I work for you while we're here." Ivor joins the conversation, looking straight at me. "I know you're smart, but I'll still make this clear so there are no misunderstandings. Believe nothing you hear, and even less of what you see. You were kidnapped by someone they hired to take care of you. Your grandmother may've had nothing to do with it, but someone in this house likely did. Don't go anywhere without me. Your life may depend on it."

"Are you sure I should do anything except live in a bubble?"

Ivor snickers, looking back out his window before declaring, "Looks like we've arrived."

I instantly move to look out mine as we pass through iron-wrought gates, seeing nothing except grass and trees in the near distance. "Wow. How far back is the house?"

"About half a mile," Tobias says into my ear, having moved to see out the window as well. "This house has been in their family for generations, and they value the privacy afforded them."

"It's quite lovely."

I admit, when we pull up to the house, my mouth drops open. I thought Tobias' place was pretty big, but this place is gigantic from the outside, which means the inside will be even more grand than I'm growing accustomed to.

Which means I'm bound to get lost in it just like at his parent's place.

The driver gets out, removes my things from the back, and walks toward the house, leaving the three of us with no choice except to follow him. When the door opens, we enter the foyer, which is when I notice there is a butler.

"Really?" I mutter to Tobias as he chuckles. "A butler?"

He doesn't get a chance to respond. The driver leaves the bags by the stairs and exits the house, the butler closing the door behind him. Then, he looks straight at me and smiles, seemingly unaware of my remarks.

"Mrs. West awaits you in the sitting room." He turns around. "I shall show you the way."

Good news for me is that it's not that far away, which means I could find the front door again if I desire. He opens the door and announces us.

As we step inside, two figures rise from the couch near the fireplace.

"Thank you, Stephen," my grandmother says to the butler, smiling at me as I stand there feeling awkward. "Please, come closer."

Tobias clasps my hand tighter in a show of support before releasing it.

When I'm finally standing in front of her, she reaches out and grabs my left hand with both of hers. Nobody says a word as we take each other in.

Even though I know she's in her mid-sixties — she'd been thirty-six when I was born — she doesn't look it. Her hair is black with many silver threads through it, her eyes the same blue-grey as mine, as well as her height. I know her eyes are taking in all my features that mirror her own as the lingering doubt vanishes from her face.

"Jocelyn, is it?" Her voice is soft and sweet, matching the gentleness in her hands as they hold mine. When I nod in answer, her countenance lights up, joy shining in her eyes as she says the words I've never thought I would want to hear so desperately. "Welcome home."

Then, she does the thing I least expect her to do: she wraps her arms around me, enclosing me in her warm and tight embrace.

Maybe it's because the moment I'm in her arms, I feel her body trembling, her sniffles giving away the fact she's crying and trying to hide it. Or perhaps the sudden sense of...rightness I can't explain.

Whatever it is, I return her embrace, tears of my own springing up before I can stop them.

As tears slip down my cheeks in silence, she lifts her head and steps back, grabbing my hand once more in hers as the man standing next to her steps forward. I know who he is, but I let him introduce himself, which he does with a guarded smile.

"I'm Marshall, your—"

"Grandfather," I cut in with a smile of my own, swiping the tears away with my free hand. "I know. I saw pictures."

"Excuse me." Tobias coughs, stepping up to my side. "I should get going."

My grandmother releases my hand, holding one of hers out to Tobias. When he takes it, she does the same thing she did to me and holds his hand still in hers. "No need to rush off, Tobias. We would love to get to know you both; you're welcome to stay here as well if you'd like."

I watch his shoulders tense as he pulls his hand away. "Thank you, you're very kind, but Jocelyn and I have discussed this. It's best if you all get to know each other without distractions." He grabs my hand, smiling at them, but it doesn't quite reach his eyes. "If I could just have a moment to say goodbye...?"

Everyone including Ivor obliges, stepping out of the room, and leaving us alone.

Tobias tugs me into his arms, making sure I feel every inch of him as he thrusts his tongue into my mouth when I gasp, a hand sliding into my hair to grip it. Returning the embrace with one of my own, I match his passion with everything inside me, making it clear how much I'll miss him.

Caught off guard by the thought, I drag my mouth away and stare up at him. "I..."

He shakes his head, dropping his arms to his sides before taking a step back, sighing. "Don't say anything. I have to go."

"Tobias—"

"Please." He uses a finger to cover my mouth. "Your eyes say it all. Their reception says it all. You've found your family, and they need to be your focus. Don't make it any harder for me to walk away than it already is."

I tremble as anger, desire, and confusion course through me.

It had been foolish to believe he tried to say goodbye to me in my office.

Because it's clear he is saying his goodbye now.

"You said only I could end it between us." My hands curl into fists, but I keep them by my side even though he looks away from me. "You can't do this."

It's strange seeing a man stand taller, even as his shoulders drop in obvious anguish.

He doesn't look at me as he responds, his voice rough. "I will keep an eye on things for you at the diner. If you need me, you know where to find me, but I know Ivor will keep you safe."

I step forward swiftly and bang on his shoulders with my fists. "Why are you doing this? Look at me! You said you weren't saying goodbye. You lied to me."

"Stop." He grabs my hands, holding me still as he glares at me, eyes filled with so many emotions I can't distinguish them. "You're not mine, don't you get that? Not anymore. I thought I could do it, but I can't, not after what I just witnessed. I'm sorry."

He lets my hands go, and they drop to my sides as I stand there, lips trembling from my inability to make sense of what's going on. "What did you witness?"

"I saw you, Joce. Everything you are, and everything

you will be. You're home, where you should've been all along, and I think this will be the best place for you."

"But, you love me—"

"Yes, I do. And when you love someone, you do what's best for them, no matter how much it hurts." He leans in, placing a kiss upon my forehead, lingering for a moment before turning his back on me. "I know you don't understand, but you will. If you're with me, it'll be because you want it, not because I gave you no choice. And the only way that'll happen is if I give you all the power."

He exits the room without even a backward glance.

And, at this moment, I hate him for what he's done.

For what he said.

For leaving me without even glancing back one last time.

For shattering the heart I didn't even know I had on the floor.

And most of all, for making perfect sense as he did it.

MY GRANDMOTHER IS THE ONLY PERSON WHO RETURNS to the room after Tobias' departure.

I'm standing in the exact same place I was when he left, and she guides me over to the couch. When I look toward the door, she gives a small laugh.

"Don't worry," she assures me. "Ivor is right outside. I wanted a few moments alone with you before dinner."

I know she can tell I've been crying from the way she looks at me full of concern, yet she doesn't say anything about it.

"You're different than I imagined." I gaze down into my lap. "All of this is just surreal."

"Oh honey, I know exactly what you mean. You could've knocked me over with a feather after I saw that picture. I had to pinch myself to make sure I wasn't dreaming, and I was actually sixty-four because the girl in the paper looked an awful lot like me."

"It is uncanny."

She nods, quiet for a moment, before lifting my chin with gentle pressure, and regarding me with kind eyes. "I'm sorry he didn't stay. I can tell you didn't want him to go. You haven't been married long, have you?"

My mouth quivers, so I take a deep breath to prevent myself from crying, and give her a wobbly smile. "Not even a month. But, we didn't marry for love."

I'm not sure why I say that out loud, but it's true. At least, *I* didn't marry for love, which makes the ache in my chest at his departure rather confusing.

"Really?" She raises a brow, giving me that 'don't lie to me' look all mothers perfect as she tugs me out of my thoughts. "Because when I hugged you, he looked absolutely tortured. I'm sure this came as a shock to both of you."

"I didn't expect this, that's for sure." I'm happy to change the topic, wanting to learn more about my family. "I found out at eighteen that I was adopted at age three. I'm not sure of the specifics, other than they had no idea who I belonged to, their only information my name when I gave it to them." Then, because I want to know, I ask, "Why didn't you answer the phone when I called yesterday?"

She stands up, tugging me along with her, as Stephen opens the door to let her know dinner is ready.

"I wanted the first time we spoke to be in person," she replies as we leave the room. "It was my fault for not having Mr. Cain tell you that."

I nod. "Makes sense. You made quite the first impression."

"It's been a long twenty-eight years; making any impression other than one of absolute joy would simply waste time."

Well, I suppose I can tell Tobias where I get my insane sense of calm during situations from now because my grandmother is epitome of serene.

As we enter the dining room, she squeezes my hand before letting it go, murmuring, "After dinner, we'll talk about your mother."

"I'd love that."

The first thing I notice is Marshall, sitting at the head of the long, gigantic table. He looks up as my grandmother seats me on one side of him, and takes the other side for herself. Our plates are on the table, but I don't even notice what I'm eating while studying him.

My mother had his coloring — from the pictures, I knew she favored him with her blond hair and brown eyes — and her features were a soft, feminine version of his. His hair is mostly silver now, but like my grandmother, he doesn't appear his age.

As we eat in relative silence, curiosity about a certain topic has me asking a question before I can prevent myself from doing so. "I'm curious," I say as I put down my fork, "why you two have Mr. Cain as your attorney? He's not exactly nearby."

They both look over at me at the same time, but Marshall is the one who laughs. "We have many attorneys, dear, in numerous locations. But, Mr. Cain used to live in this area, and his father worked for us."

"Oh, was he an attorney, too?"

"No." He shakes his head, pushing his plate away as he finishes eating, then frowns. "He was part of our security team up until about four years ago when he retired."

"Ah, I see." I lean back, finished with eating. "That makes sense."

He stands up. "I've a few things to do. I'll leave you

ladies to chat." He kisses my grandmother's cheek before patting my hand. "I'm glad you're here."

When he exits the room, I stare at my grandmother. "Why do I feel as if he's not really glad I'm here?"

"It's not you."

She sighs, rises from her chair and indicates I should follow her. Walking down the hall, I sneak a glance over my shoulder to see Ivor silently following us, then turn back around as she leads us up the stairs. Opening a door, she turns a light, which illuminates a room with walls covered in pictures and newspaper articles.

As I stand there, gaping, she walks over and points to a framed picture of my mother's face. "This was taken right before she told us she was four months pregnant with you. Marshall was so angry, especially when she wouldn't tell us who the father was, and refused to speak to her."

She tosses me an amused glance. "She'd always been so strong willed just like me, and you, I'm sure of it. But those two were always thick as thieves, and he adored her. When she told us, he informed her he'd never been so disappointed in her as he was right then, because he believed she was ruining her life."

My mother's face is lit up in a beautiful smile in the picture. I step closer, musing, "It's hard to reconcile her happiness here with the sullen face she's making in the picture you sent with Mr. Cain."

Looping her arm through mine, we both gaze up at the

picture, until she shakes her head. "A few weeks before you were born, Amanda became depressed, accusing us of preparing to toss her out. I would've never done such a thing; she was my one and only child, the daughter I loved more than my own life. It hurt to see her in so much pain, so I told her I'd never kick her out.

"I said we'll hire a nanny, especially with her depression, because I knew it would probably get worse after you were born. At the time, I had a lot of commitments and so did her father, but by the time you came into the world, Marshall and her were no longer speaking. Living with them both had been terrible, and their silence continued even after you were born, until the day that photo was taken when they argued for the last time."

"What did they fight about?"

"He asked Amanda who the father was, and she refused to answer. She started screaming at us that we wouldn't understand, you were her baby and nobody else's, and to just let her be. So to separate them and let everyone cool down, I took us all out for a while. We walked around, but she wasn't happy. I asked the nanny to snap a photo, which she did, and then the next morning, all three of you were gone."

"And he blamed himself."

"He did. He still does. And when they found her body..." Her voice trembles, her hand squeezing my arm a little tighter. "I've never seen him cry as hard as he did then. It nearly killed him that the last thing he ever said to her was how she disappointed him."

It's like being smacked in the chest, for I know exactly how much regret he felt at having his last words be ones he could never take back.

"He shouldn't blame himself. He had no way of knowing..."

"Yes, well, I've told him that many times over the years, but finding you was unexpected. You weren't unwanted, but he felt like losing you and her at the same time was his punishment. Give him some time. He's having a hard time believing you're alive, let alone returned home."

That makes two of us, I say in my head at her statement.

"I will," is what I say out loud. "Will you tell me about her?"

She smiles and leads me out of the room, chattering the whole way about what my mom was like as a child, lifting my spirits.

And taking my mind off the way Tobias left things, even if only for a little while.

CHAPTER THIRTY

THE FIRST WEEK WITH MY GRANDPARENTS ENDS UP being a quiet, peaceful time.

And so different from what I expected on the way here.

Francis informs me that both she and my grandfather were only children of only children which means I don't have any uncles or aunts or cousins. She and my grandfather — my newly discovered family — are my only living blood relatives.

I told her that is enough for me. After all, understanding where I came from is all I've ever really wanted to know since discovering my adoption, and even that hasn't been something I ever thought I would get a chance to experience.

As for Marshall, he is slowly warming up to me, but is still cautious, as if he fears I'll disappear any second.

Now, sitting out in the garden, Ivor next to me on a bench, I share what happened between me and Tobias after we arrived a week ago with him.

"He's right." Ivor stares out into the garden. "You're merely angry because you know he is. You can't deny the truth in his words."

Sighing, I put my face in my hands. "I'm not sure what to feel. All I know is I miss him."

"You should tell him that."

Tears spring to my eyes, making me glad my face is hidden from his view. "It's only been a week. I shouldn't miss him. I'm not even sure I like him right now."

"Lass." He speaks softly, placing a hand on my shoulder. "Look at me."

When I lift my head, he's holding out a tissue, which I take with a whisper. "Thank you."

"He loves you," he says bluntly. "You can be angry at him for having feelings, or you can understand where he's coming from. He doesn't care about any of this shit personally; he just wants you. But, I watched his face as he stood there, witnessing you being hugged by your grandmother, and he was devastated. He stepped back because he cares and only wants what is best for you. How can he say it's best for you to stay married to each other when you don't even know how you feel about him?"

"I married him, didn't I? I didn't have to."

"Correct, you didn't. You did it to save your diner, or so

you tell yourself." He shrugs as I glare at him. "Truth hurts, but you're the one who needs to figure out your feelings, not him."

"I know why he did it." I whisper my acceptance of his words, shoulders lowering in defeat. "But that doesn't make anything better. I'm not good with feelings, especially when he made it clear that accepting this life might mean forfeiting the other one I've always had."

"Not good with feelings? Tell me, if you never saw him again, would you be happy?"

My reply is instant and vehement. "No."

"Then figure out what would make you happy, and put the man out of his misery."

"Gee. Thanks, Dr. Phil."

Chuckling, he stands up. "Look. Everything is messed up, lass. In this life and all the others, you've been through a lot. You loved this man so much, you died for him, several times over. Seems to me, in this life, you've got some attachment issues, and you're afraid to love anyone unless it's one hundred percent safe."

He's spot on, not that I'll admit such a thing to him or anyone else.

"Too bad nothing is safe in this world, and nothing is guaranteed. You might be in danger from a mystery man who has wanted you for the past six lifetimes and will kill anyone to make it happen, but I don't think he's the biggest threat to your happiness. I think you do a great job of sabotaging this life of yours all on your own."

My mouth drops open, but before I can come up with a response, he turns around and walks away.

Leaving me with nothing except his words in my head and an ache in my chest — a feeling I'm sure won't be going away anytime soon.

❦

As I LIE IN BED LATER THAT EVENING, I REALIZE THE hardest thing for me is the fact he hasn't called me.

Not even once.

Difficult because the morning he gave me a lift home from the hotel, he became a part of my daily life and of my thoughts.

I hate that I miss him, and the fact Ivor is right.

Even at my wedding, when I told myself I accepted my fate, I lied to myself.

I don't want to like him or miss him or need him.

And I certainly don't want to love him.

All because loving him means being vulnerable; something I'm not sure I know how to be with anyone other than my two friends who have been with me through everything.

Looking back on the day we arrived, I understand why he felt the way he did and said what he did.

It's because I hold his heart in my hands, and even though he said he was leaving me with all the power, he didn't truly mean it.

We both know I have no idea what love is or how to accept it.

So here I am, lying in bed, and finally telling myself the truth.

I don't have anything to give him or any other man; at least, not at this point.

All these years I avoided being anything more than a one night stand because I wasn't ready to handle something more meaningful.

The problem is, now I don't know how to change it and curse or no curse, he deserves so much more than that.

He is worthy of the me from past lives — the one who would slice her own throat to avoid living without him, not the broken woman I am now.

Which only leaves me with one thing to do.

I pick up my phone and dial his number. When he answers with a subdued "Hello, Joce," it takes all I have to say the words we both know are coming.

"I know you meant every word you said," I choke out, "and I want you to know I'm not angry at you. You love me enough to let me go, although it goes against every single thing you want, and every promise you've made since we met. And I..."

"Love." His voice is gruff, tortured on the other side of the line, but I cut him off.

"No, please don't." I take a shuddering breath, clutching the phone tighter in my hands as I finish what I called to say. "I have felt loved more in these past couple months than in my whole life. Even growing up, I had great parents, but I always felt like something was missing. And as much as you love me, you don't love a whole me, and we both know it.

"I wish I could say I love you, and that's why I think you deserve better, but I don't know what love is. All I know is that you deserve more than I can give you, than I may ever be able to give you. So, that's what I called to say. I called to say I'm not ending it, only you can do that, but that's up to you. I have to work on myself, and if you want to wait, you can wait. But if not, I...I understand."

Then, before he can respond, I hang up the phone, crying as I never have before.

Leaving me to wonder if doing this will end up giving me the results I want and utterly terrified I've made things worse.

CHAPTER THIRTY-ONE

AFTER MANY DISCUSSIONS AND PREPARATIONS, THE day arrives where I'll be publicly acknowledged as the long-lost granddaughter of the West family.

A fact which makes me nervous as hell because my whole life is about to change even more than it already has.

It's been made very clear that Ivor is to never leave me alone, especially once the announcement has been made. I told him I thought him being my guard twenty-four seven as excessive, but he wouldn't hear of another guard being hired to give him time off.

"I get enough down time when you are at home," he'd said, ending the argument.

My grandparents insist with me being kidnapped once, nobody can be sure of what will happen, and therefore, they want to be safe rather than sorry like before.

Which means when I go out in public, there is no privacy, and no more normal.

Standing in my bedroom, gazing out the window, I watch as the various TV stations arrive for the announcement that will be given right outside the gates.

"It's not as bad as it looks," my grandmother says as she walks into the room. "They will leave once they are told to."

"They don't even know why they are here. How do you know that?"

"Because those who break the rules are never invited back, and nobody likes to be in our bad graces. It looks bad for them, not us."

I believe her. From what they've told me and the things I've read, they've always been generous benefactors to many organizations and groups, including one for assisting in the search of missing children. They expect to receive the same respect from people that they themselves gave to those in need.

"You needn't say anything." She places her hand on my back as she stands next to me. "If they ask something you don't want to answer, or if it's rude, we will take care of it."

"All right. How long do we have?"

"Ten minutes. I wanted to make sure you were ready for this."

I lift my shoulders, sighing. "As ready as I'll ever be, I suppose."

She's silent for a moment, then asks in a gentle voice, "You haven't heard from him, have you?"

I shake my head.

It's been three weeks since I called him and he hasn't called me.

Ivor reports on the diner to me, which is how I found out another manager has been hired to assist, and I'm grateful for the help. I call and check in with Molly and Nicole, but it's really unnecessary as everything is under control.

I've no doubt Tobias gets updates on me from Ivor, but he hasn't called me himself and I can't blame him.

I know he's giving me the space I need, but that doesn't mean this is painless. In fact, his silence hurts more than I ever could've guessed because I'm lonely.

I'm far away from my friends and co-workers and the life I've always known. And I miss them all.

Mostly, I miss him.

"You don't have to do this." Soft-spoken as always, she waves a hand at the growing circus of people outside the window. "This is the best way to let the world know you're living and have returned home, as it allows us to control everything, but you don't need to. Marshall and I are simply glad you're alive and well. You needn't do this for our sake."

"It will never get easier, will it?"

"No, darling, it won't."

My nose tingles as tears spring to my eyes even while I shake my head. "I have to do this. For me."

And little does she know, my public announcement may coax Tobias' ex-uncle out of hiding, for both me and Ivor are convinced he knows who we both are, and will recognize me.

I can't back down.

Because until he's caught, my life won't move forward. And I refuse to live in fear.

"I'm ready."

We leave the room, and minutes later, we're standing outside the gates as cameras flash. I'm standing between Marshall and Francis, who introduce me.

I can barely keep up with the questions flying around the moment they are informed as to my identity. They are all over the place — wondering why my name is different, where I've been all these years, how long they've known — on and on. Most are deflected with a soft smile, and a 'that's private' comment, until soon my grandparents are thanking the press for coming to the statement, requesting that they continue to respect our privacy.

And when we're finally inside the house, I turn toward my bedroom because the whole experience drained me. "I'm going to rest for a little while."

My grandparents nod as if they completely understand, and as soon as my head hits the pillow, I'm out within seconds.

"Joce, open your eyes."

At first, when I open them, I'm convinced this is a dream because Iris and Dexter are sitting on my bed, grinning at me.

"What?" I rub my eyes and sit up. "Are you guys real?"

Iris tackles me in a hug.

"I guess that answers that." I embrace her back, then pat her shoulder. "Let me up!"

She giggles, returning us both to a sitting position.

I raise a brow at her, crossing my arms over my chest. "Explain."

"You've been really depressed." This comes from Dexter. "And we couldn't stand it. So we came to cheer you up."

"Yeah. We saw you on TV," Iris adds with a grimace. "The whole thing looked a bit brutal. They were real nosy!"

"Aw, you guys are the best. I'm fine, though, really."

They both scowl at me and jump off the bed. "Come on, we've got a surprise for you downstairs."

"It's not a skating party, is it?"

Laughing, they trap me between them, each holding one of my hands while leading me down the steps.

I stop abruptly in the doorway, noticing two things in

that instant: the sun is setting, which means I've slept a bit longer than I intended.

And there, standing in front of the bay windows, is Tobias.

It's crazy, but the moment he turns and locks his beautiful dark gaze I missed so much with mine, my legs move of their own volition.

The sound of the doors closing behind me as Iris and Dexter leave us alone barely registers as I reach Tobias, and throw my arms around his neck.

He says nothing, cradling my head as I bawl into his neck, sobs forcing their way out of me as I cling to him. Who knows how long we stand there hugging before he picks me up and carries me over to the couch.

Arranging my body so I'm straddling his lap and we're eye to eye, he gazes at me, his mouth in a grim line. "I'm sorry. I tried to stay away, but I couldn't do it."

"What?" I move my hands to his shoulders, relaxing as I return his stare. "I don't know what you mean."

"I lied. I am an asshole sometimes."

"Tobias?"

He lifts his hands from my hips and grabs my upper arms, moving his face close to mine so our lips are barely a whisper apart. "Your phone call made me angry, mostly at myself. I thought I was doing the right thing, but it was stupid. I'm stupid."

He kisses my cheek before resting his forehead against

mine. "I was trying to decide when I should visit and surprise you, then I saw you on TV and you looked so scared, even with the smile on your face. And I was angry at all their questions, and the fact I wasn't here to stand next to you. I fucked up, Joce, and I'm sorry, but I won't wait for you because you're going to have me by your side from this moment on. If you don't know what love is, then I'll fucking show you, like I should've from the beginning."

My eyes round in surprise. "What about your work?"

"They have my number if they need me, but I'm not leaving your side unless there's an emergency, and it better be a really big fucking deal, or I'm going to fire them all."

I laugh even as tears fill my eyes. "You didn't call me."

He moves his arms up until he's cradling my head in his hands. "I don't have an excuse. I should've called you, no matter what I thought."

"Did my grandparents know you were coming?"

"Yes, I called them after I saw you on t.v. They sent their car to pick us up from the airport."

I know he's waiting for me to say it's okay, or tell him to go away. And for a moment, I entertain the idea of sending him away, the ache in my chest still smarting from his rejection. But I can't do it because I believe he really isn't going anywhere this time.

"So, what are you waiting for?" I ask with a smile. "Aren't you going to kiss me?"

In an instant, his hands are all over me, pulling me as

close to him as possible and groaning with a suppressed desire I feel all too much of myself.

"We should go to your room," he mutters against my lips. "Anybody could walk in."

"Fuck that." I yank at his tie, sliding it off and tossing it on the floor, grinning at him. "Everybody knocks here, and it's been three fucking weeks too long."

"Sounds good to me."

With a naughty chuckle, his hands slide underneath my skirt, slipping between my legs. Moaning as he slips his hand inside my panties, I reach between us and after removing his belt, unbuckle his pants at the same time he thrusts his fingers inside me. Reaching into his now unzipped pants, I grasp his cock and pull it out, squeezing and stroking as he strokes my g-spot.

"Oh, oh!" I move my hips, unable to resist fucking his hand, my body starved for his attention as I release him and place my hands on his shoulders to support myself. "Yes, right—god, that feels so fucking nice."

He moves his hand faster, making the tension build higher and higher until I arch my back as my orgasm hits full force.

Cradling my trembling form in his arms, he picks me up and lays me on the floor with a whispered, "Fuck it." Within seconds he's deep inside me, my fingers digging into his shoulders, legs wrapped around his waist tight.

"Fuck, I missed this." He captures my mouth with his,

plunging his tongue into my mouth over and over, mimicking the actions of his cock briefly before pulling back. "Dammit, I missed you, Joce."

"I missed you, too."

His thrusts falter for a second at my declaration, then speed up as he grips my hair and holds me still, groaning into the side of my neck. He pulls his cock to the tip, tugging my hair back to bare my neck, as he sinks back in slowly.

There are no more words between us, and when he climaxes and collapses against me, he grins. "I really like your skirt."

My response is to laugh, my first genuine laugh in what seems like forever.

And for the first time in weeks, the ache in my chest lifts, leaving me with the feeling that perhaps everything would be okay after all.

But I don't dwell on it.

Instead, I pull Tobias' mouth back to mine and show him how happy his arrival has vastly improved my day.

CHAPTER THIRTY-TWO

I SLIP OUT FROM UNDER TOBIAS' ARM, NEEDING something to drink.

Usually there is a bottle of water next to the bed, but his arrival threw me off, making me forget to grab one.

Slipping on my robe, I tiptoe across the room and out the door, heading down the steps and into the kitchen.

As I'm about to turn on the light, I'm grabbed from behind, a hand going over my mouth as I instinctively scream against it, the assailant's other arm holding mine down. All I can do is kick, but the person dragging me knows their way and holds me high enough my feet skim the floor, unable to make contact.

The assailant takes me out the back door, which I wouldn't have noticed stood open in the dark until it was too late anyway.

I still struggle against my attacker to keep up

appearances that I'm panicked, making sure to take in everything I can. The size of the frame and his hand against my mouth let me know I'm being taken by a man. As we get further and further from the house, I search my brain trying to figure out a way to get loose.

Then, I remember something I saw in a movie once and I stop struggling, going limp to throw him off.

He falters in his step for just a moment, but that one instant is all that's needed.

Moving fast, I jam my elbow back into his stomach. He grunts and his hand around my arms loosen, freeing me enough that I'm able to clasp mine together. Thrusting up and back with my elbow, I catching him in the nose and after switching arms, my other elbow slams right into his groin.

As soon as his reflexes cause him to let me go to grab himself, I stumble away toward the house, screaming at the top of my lungs. *"Fire! Help me! Fire!"*

I can't see anything in the dark, and lose my footing, landing on the ground and twisting my foot.

Opening my mouth to resume my screaming, something slams me in the back of the head, sending pain radiating throughout my skull as the man says, "Lights out, Juliette."

It's on the edge of passing out that I place the voice as the one person I never would've suspected...

Mr. Cain.

Two voices are arguing as I come to.

"You weren't supposed to hurt her, you fucking idiot."

I keep my eyes closed, afraid if I open them they will notice my awareness, and I want as much information as possible.

I don't recognize the man berating Mr. Cain, but I listen while quietly testing the ropes tied around my hands and feet. I'm unable to move much, and the bed is in a dark room which doesn't help me figure out a way to escape, but I turn my head toward the voices.

"She attacked me and ran. Was I supposed to let her go?"

Mr. Cain's voice is whiny, and I can't resist a smile. I might be lying tied up in this bed, but if I hadn't slipped in the grass, he would've been bested by a woman.

They move out of hearing distance, and I move my hands furiously, hoping he messed up enough for me to get loose, but the ropes have no give.

Apparently he can do one thing correct.

With no idea where I am, I can't even hope Tobias will find me. I didn't see any lights turn on in the house when I started screaming, which means I can't be sure they even know I'm missing yet.

That I've been kidnapped.

Again.

Nobody can claim I have all the luck, at least.

I freeze as the door opens, and someone flips the light switch, then pulls up a chair to the side of the bed.

"Open your eyes." It's the strange man's voice, only it's soft and cajoling, deceptive in its sweetness. "Your breathing gives away the fact you're awake."

I blink rapidly at the brightness of the light, my head still aching from the blow; instinctively understanding what I'll see when I look at the man who has Mr. Cain under his thumb, I keep my face blank.

And as I meet his heartless bright blue gaze, in a new visage which does nothing to mask his sinister nature, something Tobias said what seems like an eternity ago comes back to me.

"It was my uncle Artemis who grabbed you in those woods, and once he had you sufficiently drugged he convinced you we were cursed, and the only way to break the spell was to kill me."

That sentence gives me the tools I need to connive my way out of here.

At least, I hope so.

Either way, if I'm going to die, I'm going to die while trying to get free. So, I do what he least expects.

Thinking of how happy I'll be when I get out of here, the smile that slowly glides over my face is natural, and his face fills with confusion when I finally speak. "It's about damn time you came for me, Artemis."

He stumbles up out of his chair, sending it sliding back as his face drains of color, staring at me in horror. "You know who I am?"

"Yes." I keep the smile on my face, acting like I'm thrilled to see him. "Aren't you happy to see me?"

"Is this a trick?" He hisses the words, back against the wall, hand white from gripping the doorknob to death. "How do you know my name?"

"It's your eyes, Artemis. I would recognize you anywhere." I want to choke on the words, but my life depends on me tricking him sufficiently. Sweetening my tone, I lower my voice as a lover would. "I'm yours, remember? Isn't that what you said you wanted me to remember in the woods? How we were meant to be?"

"I don't believe you. You married *him*."

"Artemis." His name is a whine, my lower lip trembling to make him believe I'm about to cry. "I *had* to; he was going to take my diner! I simply did what I had to do until you found me."

His stance softens as he releases the doorknob, coming toward the bed once more.

Sucker.

I wiggle on the bed, letting out a sob while keeping my gaze on his face. "Please untie my hands." I keep my eyes wide and connected with his while begging him. "The rope's hurting me."

He leans over me, the scowl back on his face, as he snarls, "Do I look fucking stupid to you?"

I gasp as his hands circle my throat, cutting off my air, his eyes full of hatred.

"That stupid bitch didn't even do her job. I hire her to do one thing — kidnap and murder you as an infant — and what does the stupid cunt do? Kills your mother and takes off with you."

He relaxes his fingers, allowing me to gulp for air, before tightening them again. It's all I can do to focus on his words while trying to remain conscious, praying for a rescue. "She hid you well. I don't know where the fuck she was keeping you the day I murdered her and the man she married, but you're one lucky fucking bitch."

Again he releases his grip, my body automatically seeking the air it desperately needs for only seconds before his hands tighten again. "Hurts doesn't it? It's too bad I have to kill you quickly, since you attacked Mr. Cain, screaming enough to alert someone. I was looking forward to fucking you one final time."

He squeezes tighter, and I close my eyes, my body going numb as he says one final thing. "Time's up."

That's when I hear someone call out Artemis' name.

His hands lighten, but it's too late for me as I finally pass out with one last question flying through my mind.

Why me?

CHAPTER THIRTY-THREE

"Come on, love. I need to see those beautiful fucking eyes of yours. Please wake up."

At the sound of Tobias' tortured words, I try to do as he commands, only to frown as my heavy eyelids refuse to follow his order.

"Did you see that? She frowned."

"You're seeing things."

Iris!

"No, I'm not." Tobias takes my hand in his and squeezes it. "I saw that, love. Open those eyes. I know they're heavy, but you can do it."

I focus, lifting them a little and repeat this twice more until my eyes open completely, where I discover everyone surrounding me while I lie in a hospital bed.

"Fuck, am I happy to see you awake." Tobias moves close enough to my face to block everyone else out, his gaze intense. "Don't try to talk, love. They had a tube down your throat until a few hours ago so it might be quite painful if you try to speak."

I lift a hand and make a writing motion in the air.

He pulls back, reaching into his pocket and pulling out his cell phone. After messing with the screen, he hands it back to me. "This is the best I can do."

I shrug, turning the phone to make the on-screen buttons big enough, as I painstakingly type out a message with what little energy I have. When finished, I hand the phone back to him, which he reads aloud.

"You look like hell. Give me water."

I close my eyes as everyone laughs, followed by Tobias demanding someone to find the nurse so they can give me some water.

After my throat is less dry from the small cup of water given to me by the nurse, I fall back asleep, my fingers interlaced with his.

***

IT'S ANOTHER TWO DAYS BEFORE THE DOCTORS ALLOW me to leave the hospital.

And five more on top of that before anyone allows me out of bed at my grandparents' house.

Yet, when I finally convince them all I'm fine, the first

thing I do is demand an explanation of what happened after Artemis choked me out.

Which is how I end up sitting in the library on the couch next to Tobias, wondering why Ivor, my grandparents, Iris, and Dexter have joined us as well.

Just as I'm about to demand an explanation from Tobias, in walks the last man I expect to see.

Mr. Cain.

Although he makes sure to keep his distance, I glare at Tobias, yanking my hand from his. "What the fuck is he doing here?"

"He saved your life."

I jump up, pointing an accusatory finger in his direction, even though my eyes never leave Tobias. "Is that what he fucking told you? He *kidnapped* me."

Tobias stands up, placing himself in between me and Mr. Cain, who won't even meet my eyes even after I turn my focus to him. "Calm down, Joce. It's not what you think."

"It is exactly what I think! He's the one who dragged me out of the house and hit me hard enough to knock me out!"

"Look at me." He holds me in his grasp, saying nothing until I do as he says. "That's it. Sit down and let him explain."

I don't know what this is, but I must have missed something important. This doesn't make because I know what happened to me; however, I do as he requests, all while continuing to glare at Mr. Cain as he steps forward.

This time, he meets my gaze and smiles. "First off, Jocelyn, let me congratulate you. In all the years I've been on the force, I've never had anyone take me down the way you did. Where did you learn to defend yourself like that?"

I jerk my head back in utter shock.

The force? What?

I look around me, but nobody looks as shocked as me, so I swallow my questions and answer his question. "*Miss Congeniality.* She, uh, does the sing demonstration..."

His eyes light up in understanding. "I am impressed you remembered that enough to utilize it, although it made my job harder."

As I go to ask what job, he holds up a hand. "Please, let me finish."

Like I have a fucking choice?

"I know I look young for my age, but I am actually fifty." He grins as my mouth drops open, waving a hand dismissively in the air. "Now, twenty-eight years ago, I had just turned twenty-two and was about to graduate from college. One weekend, I returned home a day early from campus after getting an unexpected day off, and caught my father negotiating with someone on the phone about 'getting rid of the property.' I didn't think anything of it, figuring it was a business deal — until a few days later, when I saw a picture of the suspect in a kidnapping pop up on the television."

He runs a hand through his hair, then puts his hands on his hips as he gazes up at the ceiling. "I knew the woman, having seen her around my father plenty of times, and since he worked in the house the missing child lived in, I became very suspicious."

I curl my fingers into fists, resisting the urge to look around and glare at every single person in the room, as I force myself to listen to the rest of Mr. Cain's explanation.

"I stopped speaking to my father, telling him I was going to law school across the country so I could enter the police academy. My goal was to become a detective and bust him for a crime I had a hunch he committed, yet had no proof of. A lot of stuff went on that I can't speak of, but I kept my real job hidden.

"When I came back into my father's life, I lied through my teeth to make sure he trusted me. However, years before this, the woman I knew had taken the child was found murdered, along with her husband. Investigators had no idea what the child looked like, along with no idea what the woman possibly could've done with the child in the three years since she'd gone missing. They also had no idea who killed them."

He catches my gaze again, walking close and crouching before me, eyes shining. "You've no idea how hard it's been to maintain a fake identity as nothing more than an attorney all these years, Jocelyn. However, six years ago, after extensive searching through adoption records, I located that child — you — and I kept my eyes on you. My father had no idea you were still alive, and I wanted to keep it that way.

Because my father worked for the West family, he never blinked when I became their attorney. To keep him from becoming suspicious, however, I obtained another high profile client and moved away, claiming the West family didn't really need my services that often, and I had to follow the money."

He stands up again. "I informed Tobias of who I really was, and that I wasn't really an attorney, but an investigator trying to take down my own father for murder and attempted murder. He agreed to help me, promising me that no matter what, he would keep what we were doing a complete secret. You see, I needed to catch a killer, and we couldn't fuck it up."

At this, I've had enough, but I force myself to listen, feeling sicker by the second.

"When you and Iris left for college, I followed you to keep you safe. Tobias and your father kept in contact with me, and, along with your grandparents, we all made sure you were kept alive and well."

That's it; at the mention of my father, I can't stop the tears that fall from my eyes. The knowledge of how far my father went to protect me is the final straw.

"I didn't know how to get you back here once college ended," he continues, "but when your father's unexpected death had you coming back home to take over the diner, Tobias approached me with a plan to set things in motion. I knew all about the past lives, as my father and I had some pretty bizarre conversations over the years. Skeptical as I was, there was no denying my father's absolute obsession with you in every story he told me. Then, Tobias stated his intentions to get you to marry him, knowing it would be the easiest way to get things accomplished, and as he watched you for almost as long as me, I agreed with his plan."

I jerk my head up to stare at Tobias, who holds my gaze, blatantly defiant. He knows I'm angry at their deception, but his look says, 'I did what I had to do.' Needless to say, I'm the first to look away.

"When my father saw that picture of you two at your wedding, he grew enraged. 'That's her!' he shouted, forgetting I was there. 'Why isn't she dead? That bitch was supposed to kill her!' I convince my father I'm on his side, telling him the only way we could get near would be if you ended up coming here. Right then, I knew it was imperative we get you into this house so I could finally end this entire situation. We tried to find a way to set it up so you wouldn't get hurt."

"Then..." He laughs, throwing his hands up in the air. "You walk down the steps and head to the kitchen. I hid in a closet so you didn't run into me. I call Tobias, telling him what I'm about to do as it's the perfect opportunity to grab you, only to have you end up fighting back. I knock you out, trying not to hurt you by doing so, and take you back to my father, only for him to become enraged that I've knocked you out.

"When I went into his kitchen to make a drink, I come back out and find him gone. I rush into the room to find him choking you, but he's so focused on hurting you he doesn't see me. I pick up the nearest thing and slam him in the head, knocking him out. I was making sure you were still breathing when Tobias and Ivor showed up, and they immediately took you to the hospital."

He shoves a hand through his hair, his shoulders slumping as he finally takes a seat. "You see, one day when he wasn't home I rigged his house, so everything he said to you was recorded. Thanks to you, he confessed to the murder of the woman and her husband, as well as conspiring to kill you when you were an infant. Turning it around on him had been absolutely fucking brilliant, albeit highly dangerous as well, since he would've succeeded in killing you had I not been there."

The room falls silent.

Unbelievable. His story isn't something anyone would find viable in today's world — hell, until recently, I wouldn't have thought him sane at all — but I completely believe every word he said. This man devoted over half his life to saving mine, yet that doesn't make up for the fact nearly everybody currently in this room played a role in my life long before I knew the truth.

And even if I know next to nothing about love, is lying to me what people who love me should do?

I don't think so.

"There's one thing you forgot, Mr. Cain."

Everyone turns to look at me when I stand up, and he raises his brow expectedly.

I point at him, then Tobias, Ivor, and finally at my grandparents, before pointing at myself. "You forgot that all of you lied to me *for years*, messing with my life, with no regard for my feelings. And because of that, no matter what your reasons, with the exception of Iris and Dexter, you can all go fuck yourselves."

I storm out of the room, making it safely to my room before I burst into tears, wondering how fast I can get the hell out of here.

CHAPTER THIRTY-FOUR
SIX MONTHS LATER

THE ONE GOOD THING ABOUT HAVING PERFECTED A dowdy appearance is being able to return to my hometown and work in my diner, without anyone the wiser about my true identity.

My grandparents — although they lied to me right along with everyone else — had really done a great job of protecting my personal identity, before, during and even after the announcement.

Nobody connects Jocelyn Bates with Juliette West, and I have been damn glad for it.

While sitting in my office doing paperwork, I sigh at the ding of my cell phone, indicating there is a new message from Tobias.

Once glance at the clock confirms he's right on time, as usual. Since I left my grandparents' house and returned home, he's sent me a text at nine AM sharp every day, without fail.

Today's message: *'I'm sorry. Please forgive me, love. Have dinner with me tonight?'*

It never varies much and each day the struggle to stop myself from responding to him becomes more difficult.

Most of my anger has dissipated over the last few months. After all, I understand everyone did what they had to do to keep me safe.

My grandparents, especially, because even after discovering I was alive through Mr. Cain during my teenage years, they had to continue missing out on my life in order to avoid disrupting things. Their only connection to my life was through any information he could give them and their reaction to seeing me in person for the first time had been real, as they were truly happy I was okay.

They were the easiest to forgive, and when I told them some time to myself was needed, they understood. They simply asked me to keep in touch, a promise I have kept, even though I know they have every hope I'll eventually come back.

I moved back in with Iris and Dexter, who had also been left in the dark with me, but things aren't the same.

Our friendship hasn't changed, but I have because my emotions are on the surface now more than ever before in my life, and there have been some nights Iris holds me as I cry myself to sleep. Most of those times include wondering out loud when the pain will go away.

Then, this morning Iris tells me perhaps the only way anything might happen will be if I talk to him, see what he has to say, and I hate the fact she is right.

I know Tobias didn't lie about our history, proven by the fact my dreams were quite real, and in the end, the fact I had such information helped catch a killer.

The problem is, I'm not sure how much of our relationship was him playing a part, and how much of him truly cares for me.

And as much as I want to hold onto my anger at him, it isn't fair to either of us.

I've forgiven everyone but him, and I can no longer deny how much I miss him.

Taking a deep breath, I type the reply he's been waiting for. *'Okay. Hotel at 7 p.m.'*

Not even a minute passes before he responds: *'Are you sure you want to have this discussion in a public place, love? Come to the house, I'll behave, promise.'*

I think about it for a second, admitting he has a point. Plus, if things work out, the last thing I want is to have to wait for his touch where I need it most.

'All right. See you then.'

Then, I send Iris a message: *'Taking your advice. Having dinner with him at 7.'*

'Yay! Love you,' is her simple, happy response.

Putting the phone aside with a sigh, I return to my work, looking forward to seeing Tobias again despite all the reasons I want to strangle him the instant we're in the same room.

⚜

PULLING INTO HIS DRIVEWAY, I DON'T EVEN MAKE IT out of my car before Tobias opens the front door.

As I walk closer, he stands motionless in the entryway, hands in pockets while his dark gaze focuses on my approach.

Stopping in front of him, we're both silent as we stare at one another.

In that moment, I want to do many things. The part that misses him wants to touch him, hug him, kiss him, then fuck him.

But before I even think about it, the part that wants to yell at him has me reaching up and slapping him across the face.

He lifts a hand to rub his cheek, saying, "I deserved that."

He steps back, indicating I should come inside with a sweep of his hand, which I do after taking a deep breath.

As he closes the door behind me, I'm reminded of the first time I came here, under completely different circumstances in what seems like a lifetime ago.

He leads the way into the dining room this time, seating us at the table where hot food is waiting.

I can't resist a smile after seeing what he's prepared: filets, with loaded baked potatoes — exactly what I ordered the night he slept with me as Luna.

I don't comment, picking up my utensils to take a bite, and moan a little at the delicious flavor of the steak. Neither of us talks as we eat, and I try to avoid staring at him, especially since I haven't laid eyes on him in six long months.

Problem is, our gazes lock near the end of the meal, and I'm unable to keep the tears from springing to my eyes any longer. "I'm angry at you."

"I know."

"I don't want to be angry anymore." A tear slides down my cheek, and I brush it away, whispering, "Was any of it real?"

"Yes." He clenches his napkin, the fierceness of the grip matched by his eyes. "I never lied about my feelings."

"D-did your family know? Were they in on it, too?"

He shakes his head. "The only people who knew were the ones you know about. Everybody else had no clue."

"I feel like you didn't trust me."

"It wasn't like that."

"Wasn't it? Sure, I didn't know about our history at first." Rising from my seat, I cross my arms over my chest and glare at him. "But once you knew I remembered things, why not tell me? Why keep me in the dark?"

He stands as well, but doesn't approach, and grimaces at my question. "It was necessary to keep you in the dark. We needed you to play the part, as fucking scary as that was for the rest of us. I wanted to tell you, love, I truly did."

My heart skips a beat at knowing he wanted to tell me.

However, there are a few questions remaining that need answered, including one which has bugged me for months now in particular. "Was I ever in any danger of losing the diner?"

"No. All the financials were made up."

Of course. Most of the entire situation had been nothing more than a necessary ruse. "And the marriage? The prenup?"

He moves toward me at this point, so close that if we one of us reaches out, we'll be in each other's arms. "Yes, we're married. No, the prenup wasn't real."

"So, if I walk away right now?"

He pushes a stray piece of hair behind my ear, before cradling my face in his hands. "Are you going to walk away, love?"

At the stroke of his thumb against my cheek, our lips inches from each other, desire flares back to life between us.

This is the moment I've been waiting for.

I've received the answers I wanted, and now have to decide if they are good enough.

I breathe in, a deep, steadying gulp of air, only to feel his arms close around my tensed form. Bringing our bodies flush together, he holds me like he has so many times before, his words gentle and firm.

"Look at me." As our gazes lock, he says exactly what I hadn't realized I needed to hear. "I love you, Jocelyn. If you walk out that door, I'll let you go, but I'll never stop fucking loving you. But if you don't, and you stay, I'll spend the rest of my life making it up to you. Loving you. Fucking you. Loving you while fucking you. Whatever you want."

Laughing through my tears, I stare up at him, choosing to give voice to what we both know I came here to say. "I'm here tonight because I was finally ready to hear the answers to my questions. I was angry at first, at everyone, but I understand; I really do. And...I missed you. More than I've ever missed anyone. I..."

My chest aches. I breathe deeply once more, closing my eyes while taking a leap, making myself vulnerable to another person like I've never done before.

Tears spill over, his face blurry as the words I've never said to any other man flow free. "And I love you. But, if you ever, ever hurt me like that again, I'll never fucking forgive you."

He crushes me against him, capturing my mouth with

his, kissing me deep and long before dragging his mouth away. "I won't, love. I promise."

"I'll also ban you from my diner for life."

"Oh god, now you're just being cruel." He groans as my arms encircle his neck to hold on tight. "You know that's one of my two favorite places to eat."

"What's the other?"

"I'll show you."

With a naughty grin, he swipes an arm across the table, knocking everything to the floor before laying me upon it.

No pun intended.

EPILOGUE
EIGHTEEN MONTHS LATER...

JOCELYN IS THE WARRIOR SHE'S ALWAYS BEEN. THE vivacious, fiery, and formidable woman willing to fight and die for those lucky enough to earn her love.

No, the method I used in this life to get her into my orbit wasn't one of the best decisions I've ever made. I played dirty, seducing her and blackmailing her into marriage, intent on protecting her no matter the cost.

Flat out truth? If I hadn't done that, I might have lost her anyway because with each life we lived, things became more difficult and dangerous. I never learned much about the curse during my previous lives, except for the undeniable truth of how the woman I loved would never recognize me as I did her.

I accepted the responsibility of finding a way to end the curse, never despairing even as our worlds split, our families broke apart and everything slowly descended into chaos each time.

This life became the endgame.

We would either spend eternity together... or never love each other again.

There wasn't any way I would ever let the latter happen. For six lifetimes, I chased after her, doing everything in my power to keep her safe until others interfered. The seventh? Well, this time I had a plan, assistance, and technology on my side.

I took a risk, one that paid off, even if things were a little dicey there shortly after revealing the truth to her.

Lucky? Hell yeah. I'm the luckiest man alive because *she* loves me and is now giving us both the family we've always desired to have together.

Our love story is definitely an unconventional tale, so for the most part, I simply tell everyone we were meant for each other.

And now motherhood has turned my wife into the softest version of her anyone has witnessed, including me.

I love her and our son. They are my life and like her, I will fight and give up my life to protect them both.

Our son.

Two words I've spent lifetimes hoping to say. Now, after everything we've been through, the little boy cradled in her arms is uncharted territory. We named him Derrick, after the man who lovingly raised Jocelyn as his own, and our son's birth began a new chapter in this life neither of us takes for granted even for a moment.

My chest tightens with a multitude of emotions each time I watch her gaze connect with his as she feeds him, cherishing the beautiful bond between her and our child. I've always known she will love our children with all her heart and protect them fiercely, in this life, and if we're lucky, in the ones after this.

And after he falls asleep, she focuses her attention on me, a gorgeous smile accompanying the sexy invitation in her gaze. She rises from the rocking chair in the corner of his room, gently frees his little mouth from her nipple, and after placing him on his back in the crib, turns toward me.

Holding out one hand while approaching, her giggle is soft and infectious as I grasp it in mine, tugging her until she's wrapped in my embrace. Without missing a beat, her gaze remains on mine as she steps up on tip toe and slides her arms around my neck, her soft lips pressing against mine.

"Six weeks and one day," she whispers after a few long, slow kisses. "You better take advantage of the all clear from the doctor before our son wants to eat again."

As she slides one hand down the center of my bare chest and past the waistband of my pants, I grab her wrist and lift her hand to my mouth. Kissing the back, I chuckle as she pouts, and let go with a nod toward the crib. "Give me a moment."

She grins, stepping to the side, and I stride toward where my son lies sleeping, leaning in to kiss his forehead. Then, after caressing his little cheek and enjoying the way he sighs a bit, I turn up the monitor before returning my attention to where Joce stands in the doorway.

Her wild hair hangs around her shoulders, her lips swollen from our kisses, and when I take a step in that direction, she unties the belt of her robe. The silk material slips off her shoulders to the floor, revealing every delicious womanly curve of her body to my gaze, and my cock responds with a need only she can meet.

Then, with a playfulness that has only grown since we met, she pivots and takes off down the hallway, her lighthearted laughter the most beautiful sound I've ever heard.

Of course, not even a second passes before I give chase, eager to once again make love with the woman nothing will prevent me from loving until the day I die and beyond.

THE END!

Thanks for reading! I hope you enjoyed Jocelyn and Tobias' love story! If you have the time, please leave a rating and a review on the site you purchased this ebook from, I would appreciate your feedback so much!

ABOUT THE AUTHOR

Violet Haze is a big fan of romance — writing & reading.
The autistic mother of one, she currently spends her days
writing, reading, procrastinating, doing homework in
preparation for nursing school, & listening to her son play
video games she doesn't understand, at all.

For information on other books you can read, including
links to ALL the vendors, visit her website:
www.authorviolethaze.com!

Want to contact Violet?
Email her at: violet@authorviolethaze.com